Carved
IN
TIMBER RIDGE

KELSEY KARSON

CONTENTS

INTRODUCTION

She came home searching for answers. She found her destiny instead.

Aleece Reeves never quite belonged anywhere, not in the shifter town that raised her, and not in the human world where she went to college. As the adopted human daughter of Timber Ridge's mayor, she's spent her whole life caught between two worlds. Now, graduated from college, she's back home for good, and more lost than ever.

When bear shifter Charles Monroe shows up to fix her father's burst pipes on a freezing January morning, the instant connection between them takes her breath away. Charles is everything she didn't know she needed: patient, kind, and building his dream home with his own two hands. Working alongside him on his renovation project, she finally feels like she's found where she belongs.

Just as Aleece begins to imagine a future in Timber Ridge and with Charles, her biological father appears, bringing devastating truths about her past. Now she must choose between life in the city and the terrifying possibility of loving a bear shifter who could break her heart.

INTRODUCTION

Sometimes the bravest choice isn't running away, it's standing still and building something that lasts.

CHAPTER I
COMING HOME

T he town limit sign appeared through the light snow flurries like an old friend waving hello. Aleece eased off the gas pedal, slowing as she took in the familiar sight. *Home.*

The word should have brought comfort, but instead, her stomach twisted with an uncomfortable mix of relief and dread. She'd been making this drive every weekend for four years and knew every curve of the mountain road, but this time was different. This time, she was finally moving back home. It had been four long years, but this time, as she drove into town, she was a returning resident, not a visitor.

The thought made her grip the steering wheel tighter as she navigated down Main Street. Timber Ridge looked picture-perfect in the winter afternoon light. It was the kind of small mountain town that belonged on a postcard. Storefronts lined both sides of the street, their awnings dusted with fresh snow. Warm lights glowed from the shop windows already decorated for Valentine's Day, though it was only mid-January. Mrs. Appleton was hanging a new sign at the diner. Ricky was shoveling the sidewalk in front of his dad's hardware store, his breath forming clouds in the cold air.

He looked up as she passed, raising his shovel in greeting. She waved back automatically, her chest tightening. Everyone knew her here. They'd watched her grow up, asked about college every time she came home for the weekend. They'd all be asking about her plans now, about what came next. The problem was, she didn't have an answer.

Aleece turned into the residential area where she'd grown up. The houses were older, well-maintained, with large yards and that established feel that came from generations of families putting down roots. She'd always loved the neighborhood. The way the neighbors actually talked to each other, kids still played outside even in the winter, and the way everyone looked out for each other. But lately, she'd started to wonder if that closeness was comforting or suffocating.

Her father's house came into view. A two-story craftsman with a wide front porch and a porch swing where she'd spent countless summer evenings. The sight of it made her throat tight. Her father, Mayor Thomas Reeves, had already shoveled the driveway and scattered salt on the walkway. The light by the door was on even though the sun wasn't down, a beacon welcoming her home.

She pulled into the driveway and shut off the engine, sitting for a moment in the sudden silence. Through the front window, she could see movement. Dad was likely watching for her and probably had been for the past hour, knowing him.

The front door opened before she could even grab her purse. Dad stepped onto the porch, and the smile on his face made her eyes sting with unexpected tears. He was a big man with broad shoulders and kind eyes that crinkled at the corners. His dark hair was graying at the temples. She wasn't certain when that had happened.

"There's my girl," he called out, already heading down the steps despite the cold. He wasn't wearing a coat, just his usual sweater and jeans. Shifters ran hot. The January chill didn't bother him the way it did her.

She climbed out of the car, and before she could say anything, he had pulled her into one of his tight hugs. The kind that lifted her off

2

her feet and squeezed the air from her lungs in the best way possible, while also making her feel safe and that everything would be okay.

"Hi, Dad," she mumbled against his shoulder, breathing in the familiar scent of him that reminded her of home.

"Welcome back, sweetheart." He set her down but kept his hand on her shoulders, studying her face. His smile faltered slightly. "You look tired."

"Six-hour drive," she deflected, but she knew that wasn't what he meant. The exhaustion went deeper than a long drive. It had been building for months. Through finals, the stress of graduation, and the slow realization that finishing college didn't magically provide her with answers about her future.

"Well, let's get you inside and warmed up. I made your favorite, beef stew. It has been simmering all day." Thomas grabbed two suitcases from her back seat like they weighed nothing. "We can unload the rest later."

"Dad, I can carry—"

"I know you can, but humor your old man."

She grabbed her backpack and followed him up the walk, her boots crunching on the salt crystals. The porch swing swayed slightly in the breeze, and she remembered sitting there a few months ago, telling her father about her classes and how she couldn't wait to be home for good.

Graduation had come and gone, but her lease hadn't been up until the fifteenth of January. She'd spent the holidays in Timber Ridge in a weird limbo. She was done with school but not quite home. All of the limbo gave her time to overthink her future.

Inside the house was exactly as she remembered, though the Christmas decorations that had been up when she went to pack her apartment were now down. Warm and cluttered in a comfortable way, with her father's collection of books on the shelves and photos covering every available surface. Photos of her first day of school, soccer games, prom, high school graduation, and most recently, college graduation. A whole life documented.

3

She set her backpack down by the stairs and stood in the entryway, suddenly overwhelmed by the weight of everything. This house, the town, and the life waiting for her. She'd wanted to come home so badly during college. She had counted down the days to each weekend visit. So why did she feel like she couldn't breathe now that she was here?

"Aleece?"

She blinked, realizing her father was watching her with concern. "Sorry, just...processing, I guess."

"It's a big change." He set her suitcase down at the base of the stairs. "But you've got time to adjust. No rush on anything."

Except she felt like there was a rush. She was twenty-two years old with a degree in business administration and no clear direction. She couldn't just live in her childhood bedroom indefinitely, working part-time at the diner as she had in high school.

"Go ahead and get settled," he said, his voice gentle. "Dinner will be ready soon. Your room is all made up."

She nodded, grabbed her backpack, and one of the suitcases. The stairs creaked in the familiar way as she climbed to the second floor. Her room was at the end of the hall. The same room she'd had since her father had brought her home as a baby.

She pushed open the door and had to smile despite the swirling thoughts. Her father had clearly been busy. The room was spotless, her bed made with fresh sheets, and there were fresh flowers, winter jasmine, her favorite, in the vase on the dresser.

Her bookshelf still held her childhood favorites alongside college textbooks. Her desk sat under the window that looked out over the backyard, the same desk where she'd done her homework, filled out college applications, and written countless papers during weekend visits home. Everything was the same, yet it was all so different at the same time.

She set her suitcase on the bed and moved to the window. The backyard was blanketed in snow, the old oak tree bare-branched against the gray sky. Beyond the fence, she could see the mountains that cradled Timber Ridge, their peaks disappearing into low clouds.

She'd missed this view. During college, she kept it in mind during every stressful moment, especially when she was homesick or felt like she didn't quite fit in with her classmates, who didn't understand why she went home every single weekend. But now that she was here, looking at it in person instead of in her memory, she felt uncertain. Trapped almost, but that wasn't quite right. Like the view was asking her a question, she didn't know how to answer.

A soft knock on the door made her turn, and her father stood there, hands in his pockets, with that concerned dad expression on his face.

"You okay, sweetheart?"

She forced a smile. "Yeah, just tired. Long day."

She could tell from the way his eyebrows pulled together that he didn't buy it, but he didn't push. That was one of the things she loved about him. He gave her space to figure things out on her own, but he was always there when she needed him.

"I've been meaning to ask," he said, leaning against the doorframe. "How's the job search going? You mentioned some applications the last time we talked."

There it was, the question she'd been dreading.

"I've um...I've applied to a few places." She turned back to her suitcase, unzipping it so she wouldn't have to look at him. "I sent my resume to the county office. They have an opening in the administrative office. I also sent it to the A-Z accounting here in town. I saw that Mr. Ross is looking for a business manager. I know I don't have the experience, but—"

"Both solid opportunities." His voice was warm with pride. "County jobs have good benefits, and Mr. Ross, you did your internship with him."

"Yeah." She pulled out a stack of sweaters, buying time. "I also applied to a couple of places in the city. Just...you know, keeping my options open."

The silence that followed was heavy. She risked a glance back at her father and saw that his expression had shifted. Still supportive, but with an underlying sadness that made her chest ache.

"The city," he repeated carefully. "That's a good idea. Cast a wide net."

"Dad—"

"No, really. You should explore all of your options. You worked hard for that degree and graduated with honors. You shouldn't limit yourself." He was trying so hard to sound encouraging, but she could hear the disappointment underneath.

She set the sweaters down and turned to face him fully. "I don't know what I want yet. I need to figure things out."

"Of course you do. You just graduated. Nobody expects you to have it all figured out right away." He crossed his arms over his broad chest. His version of keeping himself from reaching out to fix things. "But I need to ask, are you happy to be home? Or do you feel like you have to be here?"

The question hit harder than she expected. "I don't know," she admitted quietly. "I missed this place so much while I was at school. Every weekend I was here, I dreaded going back. But now that I'm here for good..." Her words trailed off, not sure how to finish.

"Now that you're here, it feels different," he finished for her.

"Yeah." Relief flooded through her that he understood. "Is that terrible? You took me in when nobody else wanted me, and you gave me everything. Yet, I'm standing here wondering if I can actually build a life in Timber Ridge."

He crossed the room and pulled her into a hug, gentler this time. "That's not terrible, it's honest. Aleece, you don't owe me anything. Not your whole life, not your future. I took you in because I wanted to. You needed a home, and I had one to give. That doesn't mean you're obligated to stay here forever."

She pressed her face against his shoulder, fighting back tears. "But what if I leave and I'm miserable? What if I stay and I'm miserable? How do I know which choice is right?"

6

"You don't. Not yet." He pulled back, cupping her face in his big hands. "But you've got time to figure it out. Send out those applications and see what happens. Maybe you'll get the perfect job here in town. Maybe you'll get an offer in the city that's too good to pass up. Or maybe something completely different will happen. Either way, you don't have to decide today."

She nodded, blinking back tears. "I'm scared I'll make the wrong choice."

"Then you'll make a different choice. That's the thing about life, sweetheart. Very few decisions are permanent." His smile was soft. "Except for adopting kids. That one's pretty permanent, but even that turned out pretty well."

Despite everything, she laughed. "Pretty well?"

"Okay, amazingly well. You turned out perfect." He kissed her forehead. "Now, come on. Let's eat. You can unpack later. Or tomorrow. Or next week. The suitcases aren't going anywhere."

Dinner was comfortable in a way that only came from years of shared meals. Dad ladled out generous portions of beef stew. All it took was one bite to remind her how delicious his cooking was. Throughout dinner, the conversation was easy. He filled her in on the town gossip. The clan alpha, Nico, found his mate at Christmas, and Maddie was making herself an essential part of the clan.

"Can you believe Maddie convinced me to have the town sponsor a Valentine's Day decorating contest? All the storefronts can enter by decorating their shopfronts, and residents will vote for their favorites."

"What's the prize?"

"Gift certificates to a bunch of stores in town, a beautiful handmade quilt donated by Kate from the general store. Then, each month this year, we're doing a different theme window display competition, with the town picking a winner each time. Then at the Christmas festival, we'll draw one final winner. We haven't announced the grand prize yet since some of it is still in the works." He shook his head. "Maddie and her event planning business have really taken off, but she's always got these great ideas for the community as well. I've asked her to help with the Christmas festival."

"Seems like she is the perfect mate for Nico." She brought a spoonful of beef stew to her lips before smirking.

"What's the smirk for?" he asked.

"Maddie isn't just good for Nico. Seems like she's got you wrapped around her little finger, too."

"How's that?"

"Really, Dad?" She took a piece of the fresh Italian bread he'd placed in the center of the table and buttered it. "Maddie's been here a month, and she's already got the town and the mayor doing more community engagement."

"Maddie and Nico also convinced the county to finally repave Main Street." He took a bite of the stew before glancing up at her. "I don't know how she does it, but she's very convincing. You can't say no to her."

"I see." She dunked her bread into the bowl, allowing it to soak up some of the delicious broth.

"So..." Dad's tone turned careful. "Any idea what you're looking for in a job? Besides a paycheck, I mean."

There it was. Just like that, the conversation turned serious. "I don't know. Something that matters. I didn't spend four years studying business just to push papers around."

"The county position would involve some community outreach," he offered. "Working with local programs and all sorts of things."

"Yeah, that could be good." She stared into her soup. "But the city jobs...they're with bigger companies. More room for advancement and better pay."

"Also, more hours, a longer commute, and a higher cost of living."

"I know." She sighed. "See? This is what I mean. Every option has pros and cons. How do people make these decisions?"

Thomas was quiet for a moment, then said, "Can I tell you something? You don't have to agree with me, but...hear me out."

"Of course." She looked up at him.

"When I was younger, I had opportunities to leave Timber Ridge. Good opportunities. There was a construction company in Denver that wanted to hire me, back before I went into politics. Big money, important projects." He leaned back in his chair, his gaze distant. "I turned them down because I knew, in my gut, that I belonged here. This town, these people, these mountains, they were my place, and I've never regretted that choice, not for a single day."

"But?" she prompted, sensing there was more.

"But that was *my* choice, based on what *I* needed. You're not me, sweetheart. You might need something different or somewhere different." His gaze found hers, serious but loving all at once. "Don't stay here because you think it's what I want. Don't stay here out of obligation or guilt. Stay because you can't imagine being anywhere else. Anything less than that, and you'll always wonder what if."

She felt her throat tighten. "What if I don't know? What if I can imagine being happy in both places?"

"Then you pick one and see what happens. If it doesn't work out, you'll figure something else out." He smiled. "You're twenty-two, Aleece. You've got time to make mistakes and change your mind."

She nodded, but the knot in her stomach didn't loosen. Time felt both infinite and terrifyingly short. She could spend years making the wrong choice before realizing it.

I t was late, but Aleece couldn't sleep. Usually, when she had trouble sleeping, a nice hot cup of tea helped, but tonight she found herself with a mug of hot chocolate standing by the window looking out at the snow-covered neighborhood.

A few houses down, she could see the lights still on in the Patterson house. The teenage daughter was probably up late studying, just like Aleece used to do. Across the street, old Mr. Mason was out on his porch in his bathrobe, smoking his evening pipe despite the cold. He'd been doing that for as long as she could remember. Some things in Timber Ridge never changed.

She pressed her forehead against the cool glass. Four years ago, leaving for college had felt like an adventure. She'd been so ready to experience the world beyond Timber Ridge, to prove she could make it in the human world even though shifters raised her.

She'd made it. She'd gotten good grades, made friends, and learned to navigate a city where nobody knew her name. But she'd also been homesick in a way that felt like a physical ache. Every Friday afternoon, she would pack a bag and make the six-hour drive home, arriving just in time for dinner with her father. Every Sunday evening, she'd make the drive back, already counting down the days until she could return.

Her human friends had thought she was crazy. "Don't you want to stay for the parties?" they'd ask. "Don't you want to have a college experience?"

But they didn't understand. They had families they could call, siblings they could text, and parents who visited. Aleece only had her father, and he was in Timber Ridge. He'd come to Denver when she had something happening, but preferred to remain in Timber Ridge.

Except now she was there too, and the homesickness hadn't gone away. It had transformed into something else. A restless feeling that maybe she was supposed to be somewhere else, doing something else. Or maybe she was just tired and overthinking everything.

She pushed away from the window, set her mug of half-finished hot chocolate on the counter, and headed upstairs. Her suitcase still sat on her bed, half-unpacked. She should probably finish, put her clothes in drawers, and make the room feel like hers again.

Instead, she pulled out her laptop and opened her email. Three new messages: two automated responses from job applications and one from her friend Kathy from college, asking how the move went and demanding photos of the adorable small town. She ignored the messages and opened the search engine, but her cursor hovered over the search bar.

What am I looking for?

The question echoed in her mind, louder than it should have been at nearly one o'clock in the morning. She closed the laptop without searching for anything.

Tomorrow, she'd figure it out.

She finished unpacking mechanically, hanging clothes in her closet, lining up shoes, and setting her few framed photos on the dresser. Her college diploma, still in its cardboard tube, went on the desk. She'd frame it when she figured out what it was supposed to mean.

Finally, she climbed into bed, the same bed she'd slept in since she was five, when her father decided she should have a big girl bed. Instead of a twin-size mattress, they went shopping for one. She ended up with a huge full bed, because she was a princess and should have a big bed. It still had the same quilt Kate had made her for her sixteenth birthday, each square a different pattern coming together to be beautiful.

As she lay in bed, she could look out the window toward the mountain. They appeared just as dark shapes against the slightly light sky. Somewhere out there was the rest of the world. Cities and opportunities and futures she couldn't quite imagine. But here, in her room in her father's house, everything was familiar and safe.

She closed her eyes and tried not to feel like she was suffocating. She was home, and she should be happy. So why did happiness feel so far away?

CHAPTER 2
THE PIPE BURSTS

Aleece woke to the sound of rushing water and her father cursing. She bolted upright in bed, heart pounding, and momentarily disoriented. The clock on her nightstand read just before four in the morning. Through the floor, she could hear her father moving around downstairs, his footsteps heavy and hurried.

She threw off her covers and grabbed the hoodie draped over her desk chair, pulling it on over her tank top and pajama pants as she rushed into the hallway. The house was freezing, colder than it should have been, even with the thermostat turned down for the night.

"Dad?" she called out, heading for the stairs.

"Stay up there!" Thomas shouted back. "There's water everywhere."

She ignored him and hurried down the stairs, stopping short at the bottom. The hallway leading to the kitchen was flooded, water spreading across the hardwood floor in a dark, glistening sheet. Her father was in the kitchen, standing in ankle-deep water, frantically turning valves under the sink.

"What happened?"

"Pipes burst. I think the furnace is out, must have frozen up in the night." He straightened, water dripping from his hands. "This damn cold snap."

She picked her way across the wet floor, her bare feet immediately going numb. The week since she'd been home had been mild, typical January weather for Timber Ridge, but yesterday the temperature had plummeted. She'd heard on the news that it was supposed to drop below zero overnight.

"Where's the water coming from?" She grabbed a stack of towels from the linen closet in the hallway.

"Pipe behind the washing machine. Already shut off the main valve, but the damage is done." Her father took the towels from her and started laying them out where the water was the worst. "Without the furnace, we're going to be living in an icebox by morning."

"Can you fix it?"

He shook his head. "Not the furnace. That's beyond my skill set. The pipes, I can patch them temporarily, but they need to be replaced properly." He ran a hand through his hair, leaving it standing on end. "I need to call Charles."

"At four in the morning?"

"He's used to emergency calls. Comes with being the town's only decent handyman." Her father was already pulling out his phone, water dripping from his sleeves. "Go put on some socks and real clothes. It's going to get cold before it gets warmer."

She retreated upstairs, her feet leaving wet footprints on the stairs. In her room, she could already feel the temperature dropping. She quickly changed into jeans, a thermal shirt, and a thick sweater, then grabbed a pair of wool socks and waterproof boots and headed back downstairs.

"Appreciate it, Charles. I know it's early. Yeah, it's pretty bad. Okay, see you soon." Her father's back was to her as she watched him from the staircase.

When he hung up, and turned back to her. "He'll be here in twenty minutes. Let's move what we can away from the water."

They worked in relative silence, lifting furniture, rolling up rugs, and moving anything electrical to higher ground. The water had spread into the living room now, seeking every crack and crevice in the old hardwood floors. She tried not to think about the damage or how much all of this would cost.

Her father must have seen her expression because he put his arm around her shoulder. "Don't worry, insurance will cover most of it."

"I'm not worried about the money, I'm worried about you having to deal with this mess."

"Could be worse. At least it happened while you were here to help." He gave her a small smile. "Silving lining."

They'd just finished moving the last of the books from the bottom shelf when headlights swept across the front window. A truck pulled into the driveway, big and dark, with a toolbox mounted in the bed.

"That will be Charles," Thomas said, heading for the door.

She hung back, suddenly aware that she hadn't brushed her hair. She probably looked like she'd been dragged through a hedge backward. Not that it mattered. This was an emergency, not a social call. The handyman didn't care what she looked like.

The front door opened, letting in a blast of frigid air and a man who seemed to fill the entire doorway.

Her first thought was that he was tall, not as tall as her father, but close. Broad-shouldered, wearing a heavy canvas jacket and work boots that had seen better days. He carried a large toolbox in one hand as if it weighed nothing. Her second thought, as he stepped into the light of the entryway, was that he was handsome. Not in a polished, city-boy way, but in a rugged, capable way that made something in her chest flutter unexpectedly.

"Thomas," the man said, his voice deep. "Show me what we're dealing with."

"Kitchen first, then the furnace." Thomas gestured toward the flooded hallway. "Appreciate you coming out so early, Charles."

She took in the man before her, realizing this was the town handyman that her father had mentioned over the years. She realized she'd never actually met him. His eyes were dark brown or hazel, it was hard to tell in the dim light, but they were kind eyes. The kind that crinkled at the corners when he smiled.

His smile disappeared, and his expression went still, almost frozen as he stared at her, like she was something unexpected.

"This is my daughter, Aleece," Thomas said, either not noticing the strange moment or choosing to ignore it. "She just moved back home. Aleece, this is Charles Monroe."

"Hi," she managed, her voice coming out smaller than she intended.

Charles blinked, seeming to shake himself. "Ma'am," he said with a slight nod, then immediately turned his attention to Thomas. "Let's take a look."

Ma'am. She was twenty-two, not fifty, but before she could say anything, Charles was already following Thomas toward the kitchen, his boots splashing through the water.

She stood in the entryway, her heart beating faster than it should have been. What was that? Their gazes met, and she felt something, she was certain of it. Something had made her skin tingle, and her breath catch. Or maybe she was just tired, cold, and reading too much into a simple introduction.

She followed them to the kitchen, standing in the doorway while Charles knelt beside the washing machine, his toolbox open beside him. He moved with an economy of motion, no wasted movement, checking connections and examining the burst pipe with focused attention.

"This whole section needs to be replaced," he said, his voice matter-of-fact. "I can patch it for now, but it won't last more than a few days. You'll need new pipes installed."

"Whatever it takes." Thomas nodded. "What about the furnace?"

"Let me get this patched first, then I'll check the furnace. Could be a frozen line or the pilot light, or it could be something worse."

Charles pulled a length of pipe and some fittings from his toolbox. "You got a space heater or two?"

"In the garage."

"Better get them out. Going to be awhile before I can get the heat back on, and it's only getting colder."

Her father nodded and headed for the garage. She remained in the doorway, watching Charles work. His hands were large and calloused, moving with practiced confidence. There was something mesmerizing about watching someone who really knew what they were doing.

"You can go back to bed," Charles said without looking up. "This is going to take a while."

"I'm awake now. Might as well be useful." She stepped into the kitchen, careful to avoid the worst of the water. "Is there anything I can do?"

"Not unless you know plumbing."

"I don't, but I can hand you tools or hold a flashlight."

He glanced up at her, and again she felt the strange jolt. His eyes were definitely brown, she could see it clearly now. Dark brown, almost black, with flecks of gold that caught the overhead light. He held her gaze for a moment too long, something unreadable flickering across his face. Then he looked away, back at the pipe. "Flashlight would help. There's one in my toolbox."

She found the flashlight and knelt beside him, trying to ignore how the small space suddenly felt even smaller with both of them in it. She aimed the beam where he indicated, watching his hands work.

Up close, she could see more details. The silver threaded through his dark hair at the temples. A small scar above his left eyebrow. The way his jaw clenched slightly as he concentrated. He smelled like wood shavings and timber. It made her want to lean closer, but she forced herself to focus on holding the flashlight steady.

"You just graduated?" Charles asked suddenly, his voice low.

"Yeah, in December. Business degree."

"Planning to use it here in Timber Ridge?"

KELSEY KARSON

It was the same question everyone asked, phrased slightly differently, but it felt completely different. "Maybe, I haven't decided yet."

Charles made a noncommittal sound and reached for a wrench. His hand brushed against hers as he took it from the toolbox, and the contact sent a spark up her arm that had nothing to do with static electricity.

She jerked back slightly, almost dropping the flashlight. Charles froze, the wrench halfway to the pipe, his whole body tense.

"Sorry," she said quickly, though she wasn't sure what she was apologizing for.

"It's fine." His voice was strained, and he no longer looked at her, instead, he focused on the pipe with an intensity that seemed excessive for the task at hand.

The silence stretched out, broken only by the sound of metal on metal and the occasional drip of water. She kept the flashlight steady and tried not to think about how aware she was of Charles beside her. The warmth radiating from him despite the cold, or the way his breathing had changed, slightly faster than before, or the tension in his shoulder that wasn't there when he arrived.

Her father returned with two space heaters, breaking the strange moment. "Found them. Where do you want them?"

"Living room and one upstairs," Charles said, his voice back to normal. "Keep the doors closed to trap the heat."

"Will do." Her father left the kitchen, and from her position she could see him setting up the first heater.

She remained there with Charles, holding the flashlight, hyper-aware of every movement he made. She should say something, break the weird tension, but she couldn't think of anything that didn't sound ridiculous.

"There," Charles finally said, tightening one last connection. "That should hold for now. I'll come back later this week and do the proper repair."

"What about the furnace?"

18

"Let me check." He stood, and she scrambled to her feet, stepping back to give him room. But the kitchen was small, and she ended up pressed against the counter, Charles having to squeeze past her to get to the basement door.

For a moment, they were inches apart, and she felt her breath catch. Charles' eyes met hers, and this time she saw the same shock of recognition she'd felt. His lips parted slightly, as if he was about to say something.

Then her father called from upstairs, something about the water heater, but she couldn't focus on his words. Charles broke eye contact, moving past her with a careful precision, like he was trying very hard not to touch her. She let out a breath.

She stayed leaning against the kitchen counter as her father came downstairs and headed into the basement with Charles. She could hear them talking about the furnace, but still she stayed where she was, her heart racing, as she tried to figure out why a simple handman call had left her feeling like the ground had moved beneath her feet.

She turned toward the coffee maker. Thankful her father always prepared the pot for morning, she hit brew. Coffee. At least she was being useful. Everyone would need coffee, especially Charles, who'd been dragged out of bed at four in the morning.

Going through the familiar motions of preparing coffee, she tried to calm her racing thoughts. It wasn't just an attraction. Physical attraction to a good-looking guy happened, but it didn't mean anything. Except it had felt like something. Something more than just noticing someone was attractive.

By the time the coffee was ready, Charles, and her father had emerged from the basement. Charles' assessment was grim. The furnace needed a part that would have to be ordered and probably wouldn't arrive until the next day at the earliest. In the meantime, the space heaters would have to do.

"I've got a few more space heaters in my truck. Let me grab them." Charles headed toward the door without waiting for an answer.

As Charles headed outside, her father turned to her. "You okay? You look a little pale."

"I'm fine, just tired." She poured coffee into three mugs. "Do you think he takes cream and sugar?"

"Black, I think. Most shifters do."

Right. Charles was a shifter. She'd assumed as much, most of Timber Riger was, but it was good to have confirmation. Not that it mattered. Not that anything about Charles Monroe mattered beyond his ability to fix their pipes and furnace.

Charles returned with two more space heaters and accepted the coffee. "Thank you."

Their fingers brushed against each other as she handed him the mug, and again she felt that electric jolt. This time, she was watching for his reaction, and she saw it. The slight widening of his eyes, the sharp intake of breath, the way his hand tightened on the mug. So, she wasn't imagining it. He felt it too. But he didn't acknowledge it. Just took a sip of coffee and turned to her father to discuss heating zones and the best places to set up the additional heaters.

She wrapped her hand around her own mug and tried to focus on the conversation. But her attention kept drifting to Charles. The way he moved was economical and precise. How his voice rumbled in his chest. The way he seemed to be deliberately not looking at her now, keeping his attention on her father, the heaters, or anywhere else.

By the time everything was set up, the sky outside was starting to lighten. Dawn was coming, gray and cold. Charles packed up his tools.

"How about you join us for breakfast?" Thomas offered.

"I've got another call at seven," he explained. "The general store's water heater went out."

"Of course it did," her father said. "Systems all around town are likely failing in this cold. You're going to be busy."

"That's how it goes." Charles hefted his toolbox and headed for the door. At the threshold, he paused, and for just a second, his gaze found hers across the room.

The look in his eyes was complicated, longing, confusion, and something that looked almost like pain. Then, he turned and walked out the door. She stood there until she could hear his truck starting up and pulling out of the driveway.

"Well," her father said, breaking the silence. "That could have been worse."

"Yeah." Her voice sounded distant to her own ears.

He gave her a long look. "You sure you're okay?"

"I'm fine. Just...that was weird, right? The whole situation?"

"Waking up to burst pipes at four in the morning? Yeah, that's pretty weird."

That wasn't what she meant, but she didn't correct him. How could she explain the strange connection she'd felt with a man she'd just met? The way her skin still tingled where his hand had brushed hers. The way her heart was still beating too fast.

"I'm going to try to get a couple more hours of sleep," she said instead. "Unless you need help cleaning up?"

"Go on. I'll handle it." Thomas was still watching her with that knowing look that made her nervous. "Charles will be back later this week to finish the repairs. You'll probably see him around."

"Okay." She headed for the stairs, very aware that her father was reading way too much into whatever he thought he'd seen.

In her room, she closed the door and leaned against it, eyes closed. The space heater her father had brought up was humming in the corner, slowly warming the air. She climbed back into bed, but she knew she wouldn't sleep. Her mind was too busy replaying every moment of the last hour. The way Charles had looked at her. The electric feeling when they'd touched. The careful way he'd avoided her after the first shock of connection.

She didn't believe in love at first sight. That was fairy tale nonsense, the kind of thing that happened in movies, not in real life. But something had happened in that kitchen, and she couldn't explain it. She wasn't sure she even wanted to.

Outside, the sky grew lighter, gray dawn breaking over Timber

Ridge. The temperature continued to drop. Somewhere in town, Charles was probably dealing with another burst pipe or broken furnace, another emergency. Was he thinking about her, too? Or had she imagined the whole thing?

She pulled her covers up to her chin and stared at the ceiling, watching the shadows shift as the sun slowly rose. She'd been home for a week, and already everything felt different. Or maybe she was the one who was different. Or she was just tired, cold, and making something out of nothing.

CHAPTER 3
AN AWKWARD LUNCH

Three days after the pipes burst, Aleece was still trying to convince herself that the strange connection she'd felt had been a product of exhaustion, cold, and stress. She'd been tired, disoriented, and thrown off balance by the emergency. There was nothing special about Charles except that he was good at fixing things and happened to be attractive.

She'd almost succeeded in believing it until Charles returned to do the permanent repairs. The moment she heard his truck pull into the driveway at nine in the morning, her heart started racing like she'd run a marathon.

"That'll be Charles," her father said from the kitchen table, where he was reviewing some paperwork from the town council. "Could you let him in? I need to finish this."

She set her coffee mug down on the table and headed for the door. As she did, she tried to ignore the flutter of nerves in her stomach. This was ridiculous. She was twenty-two years old, college-educated, perfectly capable of having a normal conversation with a handyman who'd come to fix the pipes.

She opened the door before he could knock. Charles stood on the porch, toolbox in hand, wearing the same canvas jacket as before over a faded flannel shirt. His dark hair was slightly damp, like he'd just showered, and she caught the scent of soap and something woodsy.

"Morning," he said, his voice carefully neutral.

"Hi. Come in." She stepped back to let him pass, fully aware of the small space between them as he moved through the doorway.

For a split second, their gazes met. Aleece felt the same jolt of connection, like a hook catching behind her ribs and pulling. He quickly looked away, his jaw tight.

"Thomas around?" he asked.

"In the kitchen. But he's reviewing some paperwork from the city council." Without waiting for him to respond, she led him toward the kitchen, hyperaware of him following behind her. She could feel his presence, as if he were radiating heat even from a few feet away.

In the kitchen, her father looked up and smiled. "Charles. Thanks for coming back."

"No problem." He set his toolbox down and knelt by the washing machine, examining the temporary patch he'd put in place.

She hovered near the counter, unsure what to do with herself. She should probably leave and let Charles work in peace. But something kept her rooted in place, watching as he pulled out the damaged sections of pipe and examined the connections.

"This shouldn't take more than a couple of hours," Charles said, more to her father than to her. "I'll need to shut off the water."

"Do what you need to do."

Charles nodded and stood, brushing past her to get to his toolbox. This time, the touch was unavoidable. His arm grazed hers in the narrow space, and she saw his whole body go tense. He grabbed what he needed and returned to the other side of the room as she'd burned him.

It was clear he definitely felt it too. But what she didn't understand was why he was acting like it was a problem.

"I've got to make some calls. I'll be in my office." Her father rose from the table, leaving her alone with Charles.

The silence stretched out, broken only by the sound of him working. She told herself to leave, to go upstairs or into the living room, to give him space. Instead, she looked at him. "Can I get you some coffee?"

"I'm good, thanks." He didn't look up from the pipe.

"Are you sure? It's no trouble."

"I'm sure."

The terseness in his voice stung more than it should have. Aleece crossed her arms, feeling awkward and in the way. "Okay. Well, I'll just...be around if you need anything." She stepped away from the counter, moving toward the doorway, before her pride got the better of her and she turned back. "Did I do something wrong?"

His hands stilled on the water pipe. "What?"

"The other day, and now...you seem like you don't want me around. If I'm in your way, just say so."

He finally turned to look at her. His expression was dark and complicated. He appeared to be both frustrated and pained, but she couldn't understand why. "You're not in the way."

"Then why are you acting like I am?"

He set down his wrench with deliberate care. "I'm not. I'm just trying to focus on the work."

"While barely saying two words to me."

"I didn't realize I was required to make small talk while working."

The words were sharp, and she felt her cheeks flush with embarrassment and anger. "You're not. Forget I said anything."

She turned to leave, but he stopped her. "Wait."

She paused in the doorway, not turning around.

"I'm sorry." He sighed. "That came out wrong. I'm not good at this."

"Good at what?" She turned back to face him.

"Conversation. People." He ran a hand through his hair, looking uncomfortable. "I spend most of my time working alone. Not a lot of practice with social skills."

The admission softened something in her chest. "Oh."

"So, if I'm being short with you, it's not...it's not because of you."
He met her gaze briefly, then looked away. "You've done nothing
wrong."

She moved back into the kitchen slowly, like approaching a
skittish animal. "Okay. That's good to know."

He picked up his wrench again, but he didn't immediately go
back to work. "You can stay. That is, if you want, I don't mind."

It felt like a peace offering. She grabbed the kitchen chair and
pulled it to a spot where she wouldn't be in the way but could still
watch him work. "I promise not to distract you with my sparkling
conversation."

The corner of his mouth twitched. It wasn't quite a smile, but it
was close. "Appreciate it."

They settled into a comfortable silence. She watched him work,
noticing the details she'd missed before. The way his large hands
moved with surprising delicacy. The slight frown of concentration
between his eyebrows. The efficiency of his movements, no wasted
motion, everything deliberate and precise.

"How long have you been doing this?" she asked after a while.
"Handyman work."

"About ten years. Did construction before that."

"In Timber Ridge?"

"Started in Denver. Moved here about eight years ago."

She tried to imagine him in a city, but it was difficult. It didn't
seem to fit him. "What made you move to Timber Ridge?"

He was quiet for a long moment, and she wondered if he was
going to ignore her question.

"Needed a change. Needed a quieter life."

She was certain there was a story there. Something had driven
him from the city to this small mountain town, but she didn't push.
"I get it. The quiet, I mean. Sometimes the city feels like too
much."

"You spend a lot of time in the city?"

"Four years for college." She pulled her knees up to her chest, wrapping her arms around them. "I came home every weekend. Six-hour drive every Friday and Sunday, but I needed it."

"Every weekend?"

"Every single one. My friends thought I was crazy." She smiled ruefully. "They were probably right, but I couldn't stay away that long."

"Because of your dad?"

"Partly, but also just because of this place. Timber Ridge, not this house." She let out a deep sigh as she tried to find the words. "I'd be in class or at the library, and I'd just feel this pull. Like I was supposed to be here instead."

He stopped working, his attention fully on her. "But you still went to college in the city."

"I wanted to prove I could. That I could make it in the human world even though bears raised me." Her lips curled up into a smile. "I did. I got my degree, made friends, did all the college things, but it never felt like home."

"Timber Ridge does?"

It was a simple question, but the intensity in his voice when he asked it made it feel weighted. Important.

"I don't know," she admitted. "It used to. When I was growing up, this was the only place I could imagine living, but now..." She trailed off, not sure how to explain the restlessness she felt.

"Now?" he prompted.

"Now I'm not sure. I love it here, but I also wonder if I'm supposed to want more. If staying in the same small town where I grew up means I'm not really...living, I guess." She felt her cheeks heat. "That probably sounds stupid."

"It doesn't." His voice was quiet. "It sounds honest."

She looked at him and found him watching her with an expression she couldn't quite read. It was intense and sad at the same time. "What about you? Do you ever wonder if you should have stayed in Denver?"

"No." The answer was immediate and certain. "Denver wasn't

for me. Too many people, too much noise, too much everything. Here, I can breathe. I was also tired of being a lone bear. Nico and his clan opened up their homes and town to me."

"Don't you ever feel..." She paused, searching for the right word. "Stuck?"

He seemed to consider it for a moment before shaking his head and turning back to the pipe. "No, I feel settled. There's a difference."

"What's the difference?"

"Stuck is when you want to leave but can't. Settled is when you don't want to leave at all." He tightened a connection, his movements careful. "I chose Timber Ridge deliberately. It's where I belong."

The certainty in his voice made her chest ache. She wanted to know without question that this was where she belonged. "That must be nice to be so sure."

"It is." He nodded. "But I was older when I figured it out. Had to try other things first, make mistakes, and learn what I didn't want. You're allowed to take time to figure out your path."

"You sound like my dad." She smiled.

Amusement flickered across his face. "Thomas is a smart man."

They fell into silence again, but it was easier now. Comfortable. She found herself relaxing, watching him work and occasionally asking questions about what he was doing. He answered patiently, explaining the intricacies of plumbing in old houses, the challenges of working in cold weather, and the satisfaction of fixing something that was broken.

She liked listening to him talk. His voice was deep and measured, the kind of voice that made her want to lean in closer to hear every word. When he talked about his work, there was a quiet passion in his voice. A pride in doing things right, in the craftsmanship, and in taking care of things and people.

"So, what are your plans with your degree?" he asked.

She grimaced. "That's the million-dollar question. I've applied to some jobs here in Timber Ridge. The county office and a local accounting firm. Nothing has panned out yet."

"What kind of work are you looking for?"

"Something that matters. I didn't spend four years studying business to push papers around." She sighed. "But I also need to be practical. Can't live with my dad forever."

"Nothing wrong with taking your time to find the right fit."

"Maybe." She watched him work for a moment before adding, "I've also applied to some places in the city. Better pay and more opportunities."

His hands stilled. It was barely noticeable, just a slight pause in his movements, but she caught it. "That makes sense. City would have more options." His voice was neutral, too neutral, almost as if he was trying to convince her he didn't care what she decided.

"Yeah." She tried to read his expression, but he turned away, focusing intently on the pipe. "I mean, I probably won't get those jobs, anyway. Competition is pretty fierce."

"But if you did?" His voice was still neutral, but the set of his shoulders had changed. He was tense, guarded.

"I don't know. I'd have to decide if it's worth it. The commute alone would be brutal. Six hours each way is fine for a weekend visit, but impossible every day. Which means I'd have to move. I don't know if I really want that."

He made a noncommittal sound and went back to work with renewed focus. The easy atmosphere from before became charged with something she couldn't name. She'd said something wrong, but didn't know what.

"Charles—"

"This is going to take a while," he interrupted, not looking at her. "You don't have to sit here. I'm sure you've got better things to do."

It felt like a dismissal. She stood up slowly, confused by the sudden change. "Okay. I'll just...let me know if you need anything."

He nodded but didn't respond otherwise, his attention was

focused on the pipes. She left the kitchen, feeling like she'd been pushed away and not understanding why.

In the living room, she curled up on the sofa and grabbed her laptop. She tried to focus on the job postings she had started to look at this morning, but she couldn't focus. She could hear Charles working in the kitchen.

She barely knew him. So why did it matter if he got weird when she mentioned potentially moving to the city? It wasn't any of his business where she worked or lived. They weren't friends. They'd had one conversation, and half of it had been awkward. Yet, she couldn't shake the feeling that something had shifted between them. That those few moments of easy conversation had mattered somehow, and that she'd ruined it by mentioning leaving Timber Ridge.

A little after noon, Thomas stepped out of his office, and she could hear him talking to Charles in the kitchen. Her attention focused solely on the deeper rumble of Charles' voice as he responded. She didn't pay attention to the words so much as just the sound. The sound of his voice uncoiled the tightness that had settled in her stomach. She wanted to go back to the kitchen, but pride kept her in the living room.

A few minutes later, her father appeared in the doorway. "Charles is just about done. I've invited him to stay for lunch as a thank you. Do you want to help me throw something together?"

She wanted to say no, to make an excuse, to avoid the awkwardness. But her father was already heading back to the kitchen, and she couldn't think of a good reason to refuse without seeming petty.

She set her laptop on the coffee table, rose from the sofa, and followed. When she entered the kitchen, she found Charles packing up his tools, the new pipes installed and gleaming. The work area was cleaner than when he'd started, everything neat and organized.

"Looks great," her father said. "Really appreciate you fitting us in so quickly."

"No problem." Charles closed his toolbox. "Should be all set now, but call me if you have any issues."

"Will do. Now, lunch. I insist. It's the least we can do."

Charles hesitated, and she could see him trying to come up with a polite refusal. His gaze flicked to her briefly, then away. "I've got that other job—"

"At two," her father interrupted. "I know you said, but it's barely noon. Stay for a quick sandwich at least."

Charles looked trapped, and she almost felt sorry for him. "You don't have to," she said, and it came out colder than she intended. "Dad, if Charles has things to do—"

"I'd like to stay," Charles said suddenly, looking directly at her for the first time since their conversation had gone sideways. "If that's okay."

There was something in his gaze, though she wasn't sure if it was an apology or a question, but she nodded, not trusting her voice.

Her father, oblivious to the tension, started pulling sandwich fixings from the refrigerator. "Aleece, can you grab the chips from the pantry?"

Quickly, they assembled lunch, moving around each other in the kitchen as if it were natural. Charles washed his hands at the sink. She set out plates and napkins, very aware of where he was at all times. At the same time, her father made sandwiches with the enthusiasm of someone who overlooked the awkwardness hanging in the air.

They sat at the kitchen table. Her father was at the head, while she and Charles were across from each other. It should have been fine. It was just lunch, and people had lunch together all the time. But she couldn't stop watching Charles. The way he held his sandwich, hands dwarfing the bread, or the way he ate carefully, as if he were aware he was being assessed. Throughout it all, he kept glancing at her when he thought she wasn't looking.

Every time their gazes met, she felt the pull again. That inexplicable connection that made her want to lean closer, to ask questions she didn't know how to form, and to understand what was happening between them.

Her father filled the silence with talk about the town council, the upcoming Valentine's Festival, and even the weather. But for her, it all went in one ear and out the other, without being absorbed. Charles responded when spoken to, but his answers were brief and distracted.

"So, Charles," her father said around a bite of sandwich. "How's your house coming along? Still working on the renovations?"

Charles' face lit with pride. "Slowly. Been focusing on structure first. Roof, foundation, and plumbing. The cosmetic stuff can wait."

"You bought the old Miller's place, right?" she asked, curiosity overcoming her hurt feelings. "Out past the state park?"

Charles nodded. "Eight acres. House needs work, but the land is perfect."

"I remember that property," her father said. "Beautiful spot. Lots of privacy."

"That's what sold me on it." Charles' voice warmed slightly. "Can't see any neighbors from the house. Just trees and mountains."

She tried to imagine it. Charles in a house deep in the woods, surrounded by silence and space. It fit him. "What are you doing with it? Complete remodel?"

"Pretty much. Updating all the systems, reconfiguring some rooms, and adding a deck." His gaze shot to her. "Building it the way I want it. The way it should be."

There was a weight to the words that suggested the house was more than just a renovation project. It was important to him.

"How long have you been working on it?" she asked.

"About a year and probably another year before it's finished." His gaze locked on hers. "Not rushing it. I want to do it right."

They held each other's gazes for a long moment. She felt heat rise in her cheeks but couldn't look away. There was something in his expression, some vulnerability and hopefulness, yet also fear, all at once.

Her father cleared his throat, and the moment broke. "Well, if you ever need an extra set of hands, let me know. I'm decent with a hammer."

"Appreciate that." Charles glanced at the clock on the wall and stood. "I should get going. Don't want to be late for the next job."

"Of course." Her father stood as well, shaking Charles' hand. "Thanks again for the quick work on both the furnace that you fixed yesterday and now the pipes."

"Anytime." Charles grabbed his jacket from the back of his chair, shrugging it on.

She stayed seated, watching him, prepared to leave. She should say something. Thank him for the work or for staying for lunch, but the words stuck in his throat.

Charles paused at the doorway, looking back at her. For a second, he thought he might say something. Then he seemed to think better of it. "Take care," he said quietly and then strolled toward the door.

She heard the front door close and his truck start up, then pull away. Still, she sat at the table, staring at her half-eaten sandwich, feeling oddly mournful.

"I'm glad he was able to stay," her father said, gathering plates.

"Yeah."

Her father gave her a long look. "You two seemed to get along."

"We barely talked."

"Hmm." He carried plates to the sink. "Funny from where I was sitting, seemed like plenty of talking or at least plenty of looking."

Her face heated again. "Dad."

"I'm just saying. Charles is a good man. Quiet, keeps to himself, but solid with a good heart."

"I'm not interested in Charles." The lie tasted bitter.

Her father smiled knowingly but didn't push. "If you say so."

Before he could say anything else, she escaped to her room, closing the door and leaning against it. Through her window, she could see the tire tracks in the snow where Charles' truck had been.

"I'm being ridiculous. One awkward conversation and an even

more awkward lunch with a man who clearly didn't want to be there. That was all. There was no connection or significance to any of it." Even as she said it, her heart raced, and she couldn't stop thinking about the look in his eyes when he'd said he was building his house the way it should be. Like he were building it for a future he could see clearly.

She pulled out her phone and opened her email. Two messages: one rejection from a city job and the other requesting a phone interview with the county office. She should have been excited about the interview. Should have been focused on starting her career, figuring out her future, and all the practical things that should have mattered, but suddenly, it seemed less important. Instead, all she could think about was Charles and the strange, inexplicable feeling that something important had just walked out of her life before she'd had a chance to understand what it was.

CHAPTER 4
THE PULL

Aleece tried to keep her mind off Charles. Instead, she tried to keep her attention on job applications and the phone interview she'd scheduled with the county office. Even tried to think about repainting her bedroom, from the pale blue it had been since she was twelve. Anything but the dark brown eyes, calloused hands, and the way Charles had looked at her across the lunch table. Except thoughts of him always filtered back in.

It had been three days since he'd fixed the pipes, and she couldn't get him out of her head. She'd catch herself replaying their conversation, analyzing every word and every look. The way he'd tensed when their hands touched, or his expression when she mentioned possibly leaving Timber Ridge. Maybe most of all about the way he'd watched her when he thought she wasn't looking.

She barely knew the man. They'd had maybe thirty minutes of actual conversation spread across two encounters. That wasn't enough to justify the way her heart sped up every time she heard a truck that might be his or the way she found herself looking for him whenever she went into town.

"This is crazy," she muttered to herself, staring at her laptop screen without seeing the words. She'd been pretending to research companies for the past hour, but her mind kept wandering.

"I need to get out of the house and get my mind off him."

She headed down the stairs, grabbed her coat from the hook near the door, and her keys from the entryway table. "Dad, I'm going into town. I'll be back in a bit."

"Drive safely." Her father called from his office, where he was focused on the mountain of paperwork in front of him.

Uncertain where she was heading or what she was going to do, she walked outside and got into her car. There was something about Main Street that called to her, and she'd figure it out when she got there.

The drive into Timber Ridge took five minutes. She parked on Main Street and walked toward the diner for coffee. At least that's what she wanted to believe. She was going to the diner for coffee, not to gather information on Charles.

The bell above the door chimed as she entered. The lunch rush had ended, leaving only a few stragglers nursing coffee at the counter. Mrs. Appleton looked up from wiping down a table and smiled.

"Aleece! Good to see you, honey. How are you settling in?"

"Good, thanks." She slid onto a stool at the counter. "Just coffee, please."

"Coming right up." Mrs. Appleton poured from a fresh pot, settling the mug in front of Aleece. "Your dad told me about the pipe disaster the other day and the furnace issues. What a mess."

"It could have been worse. Charles got everything fixed pretty quickly."

"Oh, Charles is wonderful," Mrs. Appleton said, leaning against the counter. "That man has saved half the town from plumbing disasters this winter. It's been brutal. We're lucky to have him."

She wrapped her hands around the warm mug. "It's weird, I don't remember him before I left for college."

"He's been here for about eight years now. Moved here from Denver. He needed a change, at least that's what I heard. Keeps to himself mostly, but he's reliable. If Charles says he'll fix something, it gets fixed." Mrs. Appleton refilled a man's coffee at the end of the counter, then returned to Aleece. "Bought the old Miller's house a while back. Been renovating it himself. Must be quite a project."

"Must be."

"Have you been there before? The old Miller's place is past the start part, off Old Ridge Road. It's a big property. The house was pretty run-down when he bought it, but the land is gorgeous. All woods and privacy. A shifter's dream." Mrs. Appleton tipped her head to the side, watching for a long moment. "If you want to see it, I'm sure Charles wouldn't mind a visit. He's out there most evenings after his jobs are done, working on the place."

She took a sip of coffee to avoid responding. She was not going to visit Charles' house. That would be weird and presumptuous and exactly the kind of thing someone with an inexplicable crush would do.

Mrs. Appleton moved on to help another customer, leaving Aleece alone with her thoughts and her coffee. Through the window, she could see Main Street, quiet with only a few people running errands and cars moving slowly through town.

It was a safe town. The kind of place where people look out for each other, where a person couldn't buy groceries without running into friends, where a person's business was everyone's business, but in a mostly loving way. It was the place she'd spent four years being homesick for. So why did it feel too small now?

She finished her coffee, stood, and placed money for the coffee and a generous tip on the counter. As she left, she had no destination in mind, so she strolled down the street, looking in the shop windows without really seeing them. Ricky, who stood behind the counter in his father's hardware store, waved at her through the window. She waved back before moving toward the bookstore. It was closed, but she still window-shopped. As the door to the shop next door opened, she caught a whiff of cinnamon and vanilla. The boutique sold handmade crafts, knick-knacks, and candles.

She crossed the street and headed back the way she had came. Still glancing in windows, but more hurried than before. When she got back to her car, she hopped in the driver's seat and started it up. She wasn't sure where she was going, but she needed to keep moving. She drove down the streets, a walk down memory lane, but eventually she found herself at the edge of town, near the turnoff for Old Ridge Road. The road that led to Charles' property.

In her car, she sat at the intersection, her fingers gripped tight on the steering wheel.

Drive by. Don't stop or intrude.

She wanted to see the place Mrs. Appleton had mentioned, just to satisfy her curiosity. Then she could go home and focus on productive things like preparing for her interview.

"This is a terrible idea," she mumbled as she turned the wheel and guided the car onto Old Ridge Road.

The road wound through pine forests, climbing gradually into the foothills. She had been out this way before, but she'd never paid attention to individual properties. Now she found herself scanning for driveways, mailboxes, or any sign of which house might be Charles'.

About three miles out, she spotted it. The driveway was marked by a simple mailbox, no name, just a number. Through the trees, she could make out a house set back from the road. She slowed, debating whether to turn in or keep driving. That's when she noticed a truck parked in front of the house. Not any truck, Charles' truck.

Her heart started pounding. She should keep driving instead of being a creepy stalker. She had no legitimate reason to be here. But her hands turned the steering wheel, and suddenly she was pulling into the driveway.

The house came into full view as she rounded the curve, and her first thought was that Mrs. Appleton had been kind when she said it was *run down*. The house was a disaster.

It was a two-story farmhouse, probably beautiful once, but clearly neglected for years. The porch sagged on one side. Several windows were boarded up. The siding was weathered and peeling. Half of the roof was covered with new shingles, the other half still showed the old, damaged ones.

But the land was the one thing that Mrs. Appleton was right about. The house sat in a clearing surrounded by towering pines, with the mountains rising beyond. It was breathtakingly beautiful and utterly private. She couldn't see another house in any direction. It was exactly the kind of place someone like Charles would choose.

Her car seemed very loud in the quiet. She parked behind Charles' truck, suddenly panicking. What was she doing? She couldn't just show up uninvited at someone's house. She needed to leave. Right now, before—

Movement on the roof caught her attention.

Charles stood at the peak, hammer in hand, watching her with an expression of complete surprise. He wasn't wearing a jacket despite the cold, just a flannel shirt with the sleeves rolled up. Even from a distance, she could see the tension in his shoulders.

Too late to back out now. She got out of her car, shut her door, and squinted up at him. "Hi."

"Aleece." Charles' voice carried in the still air. He didn't sound angry, just confused. "What are you doing here?"

Good question. What am I doing here?

"I was...driving, and I remembered you mentioning the renovations. I thought I'd see..." She trailed off, realizing how flimsy that sounded. "I'm sorry. This was stupid. I should go."

She turned back to her car, face burning with embarrassment.

"Wait."

She paused, hand on her car door.

"Give me a minute to get down."

She turned to see Charles making his way across the roof toward a ladder propped against the side of the house. He descended carefully, his movement sure despite the height. When he reached the ground, he set down his hammer and walked toward her, wiping his hands on his jeans.

Up close, she could see sawdust in his hair and a smudge of what appeared to be tar on his jaw. He looked tired but somehow more relaxed than she'd seen him before. Less guarded.

"Sorry to just show up," she said quickly. "I was in town, and Mrs. Appleton mentioned your place. I was curious, but I should have called first, or—"

"It's okay. I don't mind."

"You don't?"

"No." He glanced back at the house, then at her. "You want to see it? It's a mess, but..."

"If you're sure I'm not interrupting."

"I'm putting on shingles. Trust me, the interruption is welcome." He smiled.

He led her toward the house, and she tried not to focus on the way her heart raced, the way she was hyperaware of him walking beside her. It was just two people who barely knew each other, one of whom had randomly shown up at the other's house for no good reason.

Yeah, totally normal. She shook her head.

The inside of the house was even more of a disaster than the outside. The walls were stripped down to the studs in places. Subflooring showed through where the old carpet had been torn up. Exposed wires hung from the ceiling. Overall, the place needed a lot of work, but she could see the potential. The bones of the house were good. High ceilings, large windows, and beautiful original woodwork that he was restoring.

"I know it looks rough," he said, his gaze on her while she took it in. "But it's getting there."

"It's amazing," she said honestly. "I mean, it's going to be amazing. You're doing all this yourself?"

"Most of it. Had help with the electrical since I'm not licensed for that. But the rest, yeah."

He moved into the space, and the guardedness in his demeanor seemed to ease. He touched the doorframe where he'd been restoring the original trim, his large hand gentle on the wood.

"The previous owners had covered all this with drywall. Can you believe that? Original 1920s craftsman details, just hidden away." His voice carried a mixture of outrage and affection. "Took me three weeks just to carefully remove everything without damaging the woodwork underneath."

She stepped closer, examining the intricate details of the trim. Someone had carved it by hand, each line deliberate and beautiful. "It's gorgeous. I can't believe anyone would cover it up."

"People do strange things to houses." He ran his thumb along a section he'd clearly just refinished, the wood glowing warm and golden. "But I'm trying to bring it back. The way it was meant to be."

He led her through what would eventually be a living room, pointing to where he'd removed a wall. "This was all closed off, making three tiny rooms. It made no sense for the space. So, I took out this wall and opened everything up. Since it wasn't load-bearing, it was a pretty easy job. Though I'd have done it either way because it just makes sense."

"Won't that change the historic character?" she asked, curious.

"That's the balance, isn't it?" He moved to where the wall had been, and she could see he'd left the original ceiling beams exposed. "Keep what makes the house special, but make it livable for how people actually use space now. Nobody wants a formal parlor that they never sit in. But these beams...they tell the story of how the house was built. Hand-hewn, see? You can still see the ax marks." He reached up, his shirt pulling tight across his shoulders.

She looked up at the beams and saw the marks he indicated. Each one is slightly different, evidence of human hands shaping the wood. "How do you know all this?"

"Learned some in construction, and I read a lot." He lowered his arm, looking almost embarrassed. "Spent more time than I probably should have researching craftsman architecture and period-appropriate restoration techniques."

"That's not something to be embarrassed about. It's impressive."

Charles' gaze met hers briefly, and she saw surprise there, like he wasn't used to someone being interested in his work. "Most people think I'm crazy, spending all this time and money on an old house when I could have just bought something new."

"Most people are wrong."

The corner of his mouth twitched in what might have been a smile. "Come see the kitchen. That's where most of the mechanical work is happening."

As they stepped into the kitchen, her gaze scanned over the gutted shell of a room. She could see the vision taking shape. Charles had opened up one wall entirely, creating a view straight through to the forest beyond.

"Picture windows here," he said, moving to where the wall was now just studs and temporary plastic sheeting. "When you're standing at the sink or cooking, you'll be able to look out at the trees. Watch the seasons change. See deer in the morning."

"You really love this place," she said softly.

He was quiet for a moment, his hand resting on a stud. "Yeah. I do. From the moment I saw it, I knew this was it. This was the place I'd been looking for. A family home."

"Even though it needed so much work?"

"Maybe because it needed the work." He turned to look at her, and the intensity in his expression made her breath catch. "It needed someone who could see what it could be. Someone willing to put in the time to do it right. The house deserved that. Deserved someone who wouldn't give up on it just because it was damaged."

There was something in the way he said it that made her think he wasn't just talking about the house. Was he talking about himself on some level?

"So, this is where the island will go." He stepped into the center of the space. "Custom built. I'm using reclaimed wood from a barn that was torn down in the next county over. The owner was happy to sell it. Same era as the house, so it'll fit."

"You're building the island yourself?"

"Why not? I've got the tools and the time." He pulled out his phone, swiping his finger over the screen, clearly looking for something. "Here's the design I'm working from."

She leaned in to see the screen. It showed detailed drawings. Not just sketches, but proper architectural renderings with measurements and notes. The island was beautiful, with open shelving on one side and a breakfast bar on the other.

"Did you draw these?" she asked.

"Yeah. Taught myself CAD a few years ago. Helps to be able to visualize everything before I start cutting wood."

"Charles, this is...amazing. You could do this professionally. Design work, I mean."

He shook his head. "I like working with my hands too much. The design is just part of the process. It's the building I love. Taking raw materials and turning them into something useful. Something beautiful."

They moved through the rest of the first floor, and he stopped to show her different aspects. "Here, when I removed the carpet, I found layers of linoleum, and when I removed all of that, I discovered the original hardwood."

"I'm refinishing all of it," he said, crouching down to run his hand over a section he'd already completed. The wood glowed honey-gold in the afternoon light. "White oak. They don't make floors like this anymore. Not like this."

"It's beautiful." She knelt beside him, touching the smooth surface. "How long did this take?"

"This room? About forty hours. Sanding, staining, three coats of finish." He glanced at her. "I know it's probably not the most efficient way to do things. I could hire people and get it done faster. But there's something about doing it myself. Knowing every board, every corner. For this floor, I know exactly where the grain changes direction, where there's a knot that needed special attention, which boards came from the same tree because the pattern matches."

"You really see it all," she said softly. "Every detail."

"That's the point, isn't it?" He stood, offering her his hand to help her up. When their palms touched, an electric current ran through her again, and she saw him feel it too. His fingers tightened briefly around hers before he released her. "If you're going to spend this much time on something, you should pay attention. Know it completely. Care about every part of it."

Her mouth had gone dry. They were still talking about the house. They had to be talking about the house.

"What's upstairs?" she managed to ask.

"Three bedrooms and two bathrooms. The master is done. I wanted to finish at least one space completely. The other two still need work."

They climbed the stairs, which were solid under her feet. At the top, a narrow hallway ran the length of the house, with doors opening off it.

He led her past the first two doors without comment, heading straight to the one at the end. "This is the master."

He opened the door, and she stepped into a room that took her breath away.

Unlike the rest of the house, this space was finished. The hardwood floors gleamed, the walls were painted a soft, warm gray that made the room feel both cozy and spacious. Large windows on two walls let in the afternoon light, and through them she could see nothing but forest and mountains.

But it was the details that made the room special. He had restored the original window seats, adding cushions in a deep blue fabric. The closet doors were old, with original glass knobs, but had been stripped and refinished to show the beautiful wood beneath. Crown molding that matched the downstairs trim ran along the ceiling. A simple ceiling fan hung in the center, its blades a matching dark wood.

The room was empty of furniture, but it didn't feel empty. It felt peaceful and complete, as if it were waiting for something.

"Charles, this is..." She moved to the windows, looking out at the view. "This is perfect."

"It's my favorite room." He stayed near the doorway, watching her explore. "Finishing this one space was a reminder of what I was working toward when the rest of the house felt overwhelming."

"The light is incredible." She turned slowly, seeing how the afternoon sun painted everything gold. "The view is remarkable. There's not another house like this anywhere."

"That's the point. Complete privacy. Nothing but nature." He paused, then added quietly, "It's peaceful here. Especially in the morning, when the mist is still in the valleys. Or at night, when you can see every star."

"You sleep here?" she asked, realizing there must be a mattress or something she hadn't noticed.

"Sometimes. On weekends, when I'm working late. I've got an air mattress." He moved into the room and stood beside her at the window. "It's easier than driving back to my rental in town just to turn around and come back in the morning."

They stood side by side, looking out at the forest. She was acutely aware of how close he was, the warmth radiating from him, the way she could see his reflection in the glass overlapping with hers.

"Why this room?" she asked. "Why finish this one first instead of, I don't know, the kitchen or the living room?"

He was quiet for a long moment. "Because this is the heart of it. The kitchen and the living room are for daily life. For function. But this..." He gestured to the room around them. "This is where you start and end each day. Where you're most yourself, so it needed to be right. Perfect. So, whoever lived here would know that they were home."

The way he said "whoever" like he couldn't quite bring himself to say "I" made something ache in her chest.

"You keep saying 'whoever,' like you're not sure you'll live here," she said, turning to look at him. "But you're putting so much into it. This is *your* house."

He met her gaze, and the expression on his face was complicated. Hopeful, sad, and yearning all at once. "I'm building it for...for the future. For when..." He stopped, shaking his head slightly. "For whoever needs it."

"That's a strange way to put it."

"Maybe." His gaze held hers, intense and searching. "Or maybe I'm just waiting to be sure."

"Sure of what?"

But his phone rang before he could answer, shattering the moment like glass breaking. He pulled it from his pocket, glancing at the screen with a frown. "I need to take this. Potential job."

"Of course. I should probably go anyway."

She started toward the door, and he moved aside to let her pass. For a second, they were inches apart in the doorway, and she felt the pull again, stronger here, in this beautiful, finished room that felt like it was waiting for something to make it complete.

His free hand came up, almost touching her arm, then fell away. His jaw clenched as if he were physically restraining himself.

"Thanks for coming by," he said quietly, his phone still ringing insistently. "It means...it was good to show someone. To have someone understand what I'm trying to do here."

"Thanks for the tour. For letting me see it." She forced herself to move past him, to head for the stairs. "It's really special, Charles. What you're building here."

She hurried down the stairs and out to her car, her heart pounding. Behind her, she could hear Charles answering his phone, his deep voice fading as she reached the driveway.

She sat in her car for a moment, gripping the steering wheel, trying to calm her racing pulse. The tour had been intense. The way he had opened up when talking about his work. The passion in his voice when he explained his vision. The careful attention to every detail, the respect for the history of the house, while making it functional for the future.

And that bedroom. That perfect, peaceful, waiting bedroom.

For whoever needs it.

What did that mean?

She started her car and pulled out of the driveway. In her rearview mirror, she could see Charles standing on the porch, phone to his ear, watching her leave. Even from this distance, she could see the tension in his shoulders, the way he tracked her car until she disappeared around the curve.

She drove home on autopilot, her mind replaying every moment. The way his hands had touched the wood with such care. His voice was full of pride when he showed her his work. The careful way he'd moved around her, maintaining distance except for those few charged moments when they'd stood close, and the air had felt thick with possibility. In the bedroom, he looked at her like she was something he wanted desperately but couldn't let himself have.

By the time she pulled into the driveway at home, she had almost convinced herself that the whole visit had been perfectly normal and meant nothing. *Almost.*

She shut off the car and got out. The minute the cold January air hit her, it refreshed her. She tipped her head up and looked at the clouds. Nowhere else had ever felt like Timber Ridge. It was home.

Why would I want to give all of this up?

She stepped into the house, and the minute she did, she knew her father was making dinner. Putting her coat on the hook, she smiled as she headed to the kitchen.

"Good drive?" he asked, looking back at her. As he looked at her, he grinned.

"Fine." She avoided his gaze.

"Go anywhere interesting?"

"Just around."

"Mm-hmm." He stirred something on the stove. "You know, Mrs. Appleton called. She said you were asking about Charles' place."

She felt her face heat with embarrassment. "I was curious."

"I'm sure you were." He stood there still grinning. "Did your curiosity lead you out to Old Ridge Road by any chance?"

"Maybe."

"And?"

"It's a nice property. He's doing good work on the house." She turned to the refrigerator and grabbed a bottle of water, needing something to do with her hands. "That's all."

Her father made a noncommittal sound that clearly meant he didn't believe her for a second. "Charles is a good man, you know. Quiet, keeps to himself, but solid. Did I mention that already?"

"Yes, Dad. You mentioned it."

"Just making sure you heard me." He turned back to the stove. "He's not seeing anyone, from what I know. In case you were wondering."

"I wasn't."

"No? My mistake." But he was still smiling, as if he knew the truth.

She escaped to her room before he could say anything else. She closed the door and leaned against it, closing her eyes.

This was getting out of hand. She'd known Charles for only a short time and had maybe an hour of actual conversation with him in total. There was no reason for her to be this affected, this drawn to him. Yet her thoughts kept returning to the way he'd looked at her in that golden bedroom light.

Her phone buzzed. She pulled it out of her pocket and saw a text from her friend Jessica on the screen.

How's small-town life? Met any hot lumberjacks yet?

Aleece stared at the message, then set her phone down without responding. Because the answer was yes, sort of, except he was a handyman, not a lumberjack. She had no idea what was happening between them or if anything was happening at all. The whole situation was confusing and frustrating, and made her feel things she didn't understand.

Through her window, she could see the mountains, dark against the evening sky. Somewhere out there, in a house in the woods, Charles was probably back on his roof, putting on shingles in the fading light. Was he thinking about her visit? Or had he already forgotten about it, moved on to his work, his plans, his carefully constructed solitary life?

She didn't know. All she knew was that something was pulling her toward Charles Monroe, and she had no idea if she should resist it or give in. Or if he even felt it too.

CHAPTER 5
THE SECOND MEETING

Aleece woke up on Saturday morning with a sense of purpose she hadn't felt in days. Every day she was in Timber Ridge, her life felt more settled.

Sitting at the table with her father for breakfast had become a usual morning routine, but on the weekends, it wasn't as rushed as during the week when he had to head down to the city building.

"I need to get some supplies at the hardware store." Her father brought the fork of eggs to his lips.

"For the shelves for your office?" she asked.

"Yes. I want to get them up this weekend."

"I'll go." She volunteered before he even asked.

"You sure?" Her father had said, looking up from his breakfast with surprise. "I can get them later."

"I don't mind. I need to get out of the house anyway." She grabbed the list and her keys before he could ask her any further questions.

"Thanks," he called as she headed toward the door.

Minutes later, she was driving toward town, trying to convince herself that this had nothing to do with the hopes of seeing Charles at the hardware store. The hardware store was Timber Ridge's main supplier of building materials, and many people shopped there. Which means the chances of running into Charles specifically were slim. But her heart was beating faster as she pulled into the parking lot.

The hardware store was busy for a Saturday morning. Aleece grabbed a cart and pulled out her father's list, scanning it. Wood screws, brackets, sandpaper, and wood stain. She could find most of this herself, but she'd probably need help with the brackets.

She was examining packages of screws, trying to figure out the difference between the packages of screws, when she heard a familiar deep voice behind her.

"Eights will work better for what Thomas is doing."

She spun toward him, nearly dropping the box of screws she was holding. There he stood, wearing his usual faded jeans, a flannel shirt, and his canvas jacket. His hair looked damp, like he'd showered recently, and he had a cart full of lumber and supplies.

"Hi," she managed, hating how breathless she sounded. "How did you know what my dad was building?"

"Ran into him at the diner yesterday. He mentioned the shelves." Charles moved closer, reaching past her to grab a box of screws. "These. One and a half inches. Perfect length for what he needs."

His arm brushed against hers, and she felt the now-familiar jolt of electricity. He pulled back quickly, but not before she saw him react. The slight widening of his eyes, the sharp intake of breath.

"Thanks." She put the screws in her cart, trying to act normal. "I probably would have bought the wrong size."

"Hardware stores can be overwhelming if you're not used to them." He gestured to his full cart. "Picking up materials for the house. Finally tackling the deck."

"That's exciting." She fell into step beside him as he moved toward the lumber section. "How's the roof coming?"

"Almost done. Another few days." He stopped in front of stacks

52

of pressure-treated lumber, examining boards for warping. "Then I can focus on the deck before the weather gets too warm."

"Building a deck seems complicated."

"It's methodical. Footings, frame, joists, decking. Just take it step by step." He selected several boards, checking each one carefully before adding it to his cart. "Most construction is like that, looks overwhelming until you break it down into manageable pieces."

She watched him work, noting the way he rejected boards that others probably wouldn't notice were flawed. "You really care about getting everything right."

"No point in doing something if you're not going to do it properly." He glanced at her. "That probably sounds obsessive."

"It sounds like you take pride in your work."

His expression softened. "I do. This house matters, and I want it to be perfect."

"For whoever needs it?" She quoted his words from the other day, unable to help herself.

His hands stilled on a board. "Yeah. For that."

The air between them felt charged again, heavy with unspoken things. She wanted to push, ask what he meant, and understand why he kept talking about this house as if it were for someone else when he was the one building it.

But before she could find the words, another customer squeezed past them, breaking the moment. Charles moved his cart, and she followed, helping him load the lumber even though he clearly didn't need assistance.

"So," she said, trying to sound casual, "how much longer do you think the whole renovation will take?"

"At my current pace? Another year, maybe. Could go faster if I hired help, but..." He shrugged. "I like doing the work myself."

"Must get lonely though. Working out there all alone."

He was quiet for a moment, maneuvering his cart toward the checkout. "I'm used to it. Used to being alone."

The way he said it, matter-of-fact but with an underlying sadness, made her want to change it. She thought about the beautifully finished bedroom, empty except for an occasional air mattress. About him spending weekends in that big house by himself, methodically working through his renovation plans.

Together, they finished grabbing the items they came for. She grabbed the last few items on her father's list. Sandpaper and wood stain, but most of all, she was thankful for his help with the brackets. Charles had two carts worth of materials, enough to keep him busy for weeks. Eventually, they made their way to the checkout line, standing close together as they waited.

"Big project," the cashier commented as she began scanning Charles' items.

"Building a deck."

"By yourself?"

"That's the plan."

The cashier shook her head admiringly. "Wish my husband had half your initiative. He's been promising to fix our back steps for six months."

Charles smiled politely but didn't respond. Aleece noticed he wasn't much for small talk with strangers. With her, though, he'd been different. More open. Or maybe she was imagining that.

When it was her turn to check out, she loaded her items onto the counter. Charles was already heading toward the door with his lumber, but he paused, waiting just outside the doors.

"Need help loading that?" he asked when she emerged with her bags.

"I've got it, thanks. Nothing too heavy."

"Okay." But he didn't move, just stood there looking at her with an expression she couldn't quite read. "It was good to see you again."

"You too."

They stood in the parking lot, neither quite willing to walk away. She knew she should say goodbye, get in her car, and go home. But the words that came out of her mouth were entirely different.

"I could help with the deck."

He blinked. "What?"

"I could help you build it. I mean, I don't know anything about construction, but I can follow instructions. Hand you tools or hold things steady." The words tumbled out faster as she spoke. "I'm job hunting right now, so I've got free time during the week, and I need something to do besides stare at my laptop and—"

"Aleece." His voice was gentle, stopping her ramble.

"Sorry. That was presumptuous. You probably don't want some amateur getting in your way—"

"I'd like that."

Her mouth snapped shut. "You would?"

"Yeah." Charles shifted his weight, looking almost nervous. "I mean, if you're serious. It's physical work. Lots of measuring, cutting, and carrying heavy things."

"I can handle it."

"It might be boring. I'm not the most entertaining company."

"I don't need entertaining. I just..." She paused, trying to figure out how to explain without sounding pathetic. "I loved seeing what you're doing with the house. The craftsmanship, the attention to detail. I'd like to learn more about it and how things are built."

That wasn't entirely true. Or rather, it was true, but it wasn't the whole truth. In reality, she wanted to spend more time with him, to understand the pull she felt, to figure out if he felt it too. But she couldn't say that.

He studied her for a long moment, and she held her breath, suddenly terrified he'd say no. That he'd see through her flimsy excuse and realize she was just manufacturing reasons to be around him.

"Okay," he finally said. "Tomorrow? I'm planning to start around nine, work until it gets dark."

"Tomorrow's perfect."

"Bring work gloves if you have them, and wear clothes you don't mind getting dirty." He paused. "You sure about this? I don't want you to feel obligated—"

"I'm sure." She smiled, unable to contain the flutter of excitement in her chest. "I'll be there at nine."

"Okay." He returned her smile, a real one this time that transformed his whole face. "See you tomorrow, then."

He loaded his lumber into his truck while she put her bags in her car. She tried not to obviously watch him work, but her gaze kept drifting back to the efficient way he moved, the strength in his arms as he lifted the heavy boards.

When she finally got into her car and drove away, she caught him watching her in her rearview mirror, standing beside his truck with an expression that looked almost hopeful.

The drive home felt both too short and too long. Her thoughts were racing, already planning what she'd wear, whether she should bring lunch, and if she should stop by the hardware store again and buy actual work gloves instead of the gardening ones in the garage.

When she entered the house, she found her father in the living room, reading the newspaper.

"Got everything?" he asked.

"Yep." She set the bags down, trying to sound casual. "Ran into Charles at the store. He helped me find the right screws."

"That was nice of him."

"Yeah. And, um, I'm going to help him with his deck tomorrow. The renovation project. He could use an extra pair of hands."

Her father lowered his newspaper slowly, his expression neutral in a way that meant he was trying very hard not to smile. "Is that so?"

"It's just helping with a construction project. It's no big deal."

"Of course not." His lips twitched. "What time are you heading over there?"

"Nine." She busied herself pulling items from the bags. "I'll probably be gone most of the day. He said it's a big project."

"I'm sure it is." Her father gave up the fight and grinned. "Should I pack you a lunch?"

"Dad."

"What? You'll need to eat. Can't build decks on an empty stomach."

She threw a package of sandpaper at him, which he caught easily, laughing. "You're impossible."

"I'm supportive. There's a difference." He stood and gathered his supplies. "Charles is a good man, sweetheart. Smart, hardworking, and treats people right. If you're spending time with him, you could do a lot worse."

"We're building a deck. That's all."

"Mm-hmm." He headed toward his office, still smiling. "Don't forget those work gloves. Pretty sure we've got some in the garage."

She spent the rest of the day trying to act normal, but failed. Job applications were left unfinished as her focus kept drifting. She started three different books and couldn't get past the first chapter of any of them. Unable to focus on anything but the next day, she decided to reorganize her closet. Which basically meant pulling out clothes and trying to figure out what clothes she didn't mind getting dirty. Not that it mattered what she wore. They were building a deck. It was practical, not social. But she still tried on four different combinations of jeans and shirts before settling on her most comfortable pair of jeans and an old college sweatshirt.

With her clothes picked out, she headed downstairs. She needed something to do with her hands, and maybe her father would need help with the shelves. Instead of finding him in his office, she found him in the kitchen closing the oven door.

"Lasagna," he said as she came up behind him. "About an hour until it's ready."

"Dad's famous lasagna. What's the occasion?"

"Thought you might be nervous. This is good comfort food, and it's your favorite."

"Nervous about what?" she asked.

"Tomorrow. The deck building." He turned back toward her.

"Why would I be nervous? It's just construction work." She

leaned back against the kitchen counter but didn't look up to meet his gaze.

"If you say so."

"What's that supposed to mean?" She looked up at him.

"Nothing." But the smile on his face spoke volumes. "Just be yourself. Don't overthink it."

"Me?" She smirked. "I never overthink anything."

"Good. Then you'll have a great time." With that, he headed back to his office, leaving her alone in the kitchen.

She stood there by the kitchen sink looking out at the backyard, but in her mind, she was thinking of the view at Charles' house. The forest, the empty space, and the mountains in the distance. She closed her eyes and pictured the man who actually held her attention. Instantly, she could see Charles, the way he looked at her in the hardware store, and the way he'd smiled when she offered to help.

"Tomorrow," she whispered, equal parts excited and terrified.

Tomorrow, she'd figure out what this thing was between them. This pull, that being near Charles, was exactly where she was supposed to be. Or it would prove it was all in her head, and she'd embarrass herself by showing up to help build a deck for a man who was just being polite and didn't actually want her there. Either way, at least she'd know.

Please let tomorrow be real. Please let him feel this too.

CHAPTER 6

BUILDING TOGETHER

The clothes Aleece picked out didn't fit her morning mood. Instead, she changed her outfit three times before finally settling on dark jeans, a fitted thermal shirt, and a flannel button-up left open over it. Practical, but not trying too hard. The jeans were old enough that she wouldn't care if they got dirty, but they also happened to fit well. The flannel was one of her favorites— soft from years of washing, in shades of blue that brought out the color in her eyes.

She grabbed the work gloves from the garage. They were canvas with leather palms and were barely used. Before checking her reflection one more time in the hall mirror. Her hair was pulled back in a ponytail, minimal makeup, nothing that would look out of place on a construction site.

"You look nice," her father said from the kitchen doorway, coffee mug in hand and that knowing smile on his face.

"I look practical," she corrected, grabbing her keys.

"That too." He raised his mug in a salute. "Have fun building that deck."

"It's work, not fun."

"If you say so."

She escaped before he could say anything else. In the car, she tried to calm her nerves. Yet, her stomach fluttered with nerves. This was just a construction project. Just two people working together on a deck. Nothing to be nervous about.

Except her hands were shaking slightly as she turned onto Old Ridge Road.

Charles' truck was already in the driveway when she arrived at five minutes to nine. She parked beside it and sat for a moment, taking deep breaths. She could see him behind the house near the shed, but she couldn't make out what he was doing.

She could do this. She could spend the day with Charles and act like a normal person who wasn't inexplicably drawn to him. She grabbed her gloves from the passenger seat, where she tossed them, and got out of the car.

Charles looked back toward her at the sound of her door closing. He was wearing jeans and a gray thermal that had seen better days, work boots, and a tool belt slung low on his hips. His hair was slightly disheveled, like he'd been running his hands through it, and he looked really good.

"Hey," he called out, strolling toward her. "You made it."

"I said I would." She walked over suddenly shy. "Put me to work."

His expression softened into something that might have been relief. "I wasn't sure you'd actually come. Thought you might wake up and realize you had better things to do on a Sunday."

"Better than learning how to build a deck? Doubtful."

"We'll see if you still feel that way after a few hours of hauling lumber." But he was smiling as he said it. "Come on, let me show you what we're doing."

He led her around to the back of the house, where the ground had already been marked with stakes and string. The area was larger than she'd expected. Maybe twenty by fifteen feet.

"This will be the main deck," he explained, gesturing to the marked space. "Then a smaller landing here by the back door, with steps down to the main level."

"It's huge."

"It needs to be. The view..." He turned toward the forest, and she followed his gaze. From this vantage point, you could see between the trees to where the valley opened up, mountains rising in layers of blue-gray beyond. "I wanted space to actually use it. Room for furniture, for eating outside, and for just being together."

She heard what he didn't say: *For sharing with someone.*

"The view is incredible," she said softly.

"That's why I positioned it here exactly. Most people would put the deck off the kitchen for convenience, but from this spot, you get the sunrise over the mountains. In the evening, the light turns everything gold." He pointed to different areas as he spoke. "I've designed it so the railing won't block the view. Low profile, with glass panels instead of traditional balusters."

"You've really thought this through."

"I've had a year to plan." He pulled out his phone, hit a few buttons, and then held it out to her to show her detailed drawings similar to the kitchen island designs she'd seen before. "These are the final plans. We'll start with the footings today. Digging holes, setting posts, that kind of thing. It's the most labor-intensive part, but it's crucial. Everything else depends on getting the foundation right."

She studied the drawings. They were beautiful. Not just functional plans, but something carefully designed to enhance the house and landscape. "How did you learn to do all this? The design work, I mean."

"Trial and error mostly. Books. Online courses." He pocketed his phone. "When I first moved here, I had time on my hands. Needed something to focus on besides..." He trailed off, then redirected. "Anyway. I learned."

She could tell there was a story there. Something about what had brought him to Timber Ridge, what he'd been running from or toward. But she didn't push.

"So," he said, all business now. "I've got two post hole diggers. The ground is partially frozen, so it's going to be tough work. We need holes three feet deep, spaced exactly according to the plan."

"Three feet?" She looked at the marked spots. There had to be at least a dozen.

"Yep. Building code requires it for frost protection. Welcome to construction." But his tone was kind, almost apologetic. "Last chance to back out."

"Not a chance. Just tell me what to do."

Hard work wasn't going to scare her away from spending the day working alongside him. This was her chance to get to know him better and for him to see her as someone besides Thomas' daughter.

The next few hours were some of the hardest physical work Aleece had ever done. The ground was indeed partially frozen, and each hole required serious effort to dig. Charles showed her the technique, jamming the digger down, twisting, pulling up soil, and they fell into a rhythm, working side by side.

At first, they were quiet except for the sounds of exertion and the occasional direction from him about depth or placement. But gradually, as they settled into the work, conversation began to flow.

"So, what's your degree in again?" he asked, pausing to wipe sweat from his forehead despite the cold air. "Business?"

"Business administration. Exciting, right?" She dumped another load of dirt beside the hole she was digging.

"Useful though. What made you choose it?"

She leaned on her digger, considering. "Honestly? I didn't know what else to pick. It felt practical and safe. The kind of degree that could lead to lots of different careers." She resumed digging. "I'm starting to think that was a cop-out. That I should have chosen something I actually cared about."

"Like what?"

"I don't know. That's the problem." She grunted as she twisted the digger through a particularly stubborn section of earth. "I spent four years studying something practical instead of figuring out what I actually wanted."

He was quiet for a moment. "You're twenty-two. You've got time to figure it out."

"Everyone keeps saying that. But it doesn't feel like it. All my friends from college already have jobs, apartments, and plans. I'm living with my dad, digging holes in the woods."

"Hey." His voice made her look up. "There's nothing wrong with living with your dad while you figure things out. And there's definitely nothing wrong with digging holes in the woods. Some people would pay for the privilege of doing this kind of physical labor. Call it therapy."

Despite herself, she laughed. "Is that what this is? Therapeutic hole digging?"

"Absolutely. Very meditative. The repetitive motion, the simple goal, the satisfaction of completion." His eyes crinkled at the corners. "Plus, you're building something. Creating instead of just consuming. That's worth something."

"Is that why you do it? The renovation work?"

"Partly." He moved to check the depth of his hole, using a marked stick to measure. "But also, because it gives me purpose. A reason to get up in the morning. Something to work toward that's bigger than just existing."

The way he said it, with a weight that suggested deeper meaning, made her study him more carefully. "You make it sound like you needed that type of purpose."

"Yeah, I did. When I first moved here, I was lost. Working on the house gave me something to focus on. A project that mattered."

"What were you lost from?" The question came out before she could stop it.

His hands stilled on the post hole digger. "That's a longer conversation." He met her gaze briefly, something painful flickering across his face. "Maybe another time."

"Okay." She understood boundaries. But she filed the information away, adding it to the puzzle that was him.

They worked in companionable silence for a while longer. The holes were finally at the right depth, and he showed her how to mix and pour concrete, setting the posts level and plumb. It was precise work, requiring patience and attention to detail.

"This is what I mean," he said as they worked. "This part right here, it's not glamorous. Nobody will ever see these posts once the deck is done. But if we don't get them exactly right, level and square, everything else will be off. The whole structure will be compromised."

"Like foundations in life," she said without thinking.

He looked up sharply, meeting her eyes. "Yeah. Exactly like that."

The moment stretched between them, heavy with meaning. She felt heat rise in her cheeks but couldn't look away.

Then he cleared his throat and returned to adjusting the post. "Anyway. That's why we're taking the time to do it right."

By the time they'd set all the posts, it was past noon. Her arms ached, her back hurt, and she was pretty sure blisters were forming despite the gloves. But she also felt good. Accomplished. Like she'd done something real.

"Lunch break," he announced, straightening with a grimace. "I've got sandwiches if you want. Nothing fancy."

"Sandwiches sound perfect."

They sat on the back steps, eating turkey sandwiches and

drinking water from a cooler he'd brought out. The view stretched before them, peaceful and vast.

"I can see why you chose this spot," she said between bites. "It's beautiful here."

"It's more than that." His gaze swept the forest. "It's quiet. Private. When you're out here, you can hear yourself think. No noise, no expectations. Just space to breathe."

"Is that what you needed? Space to breathe?"

"Yeah." He turned to look at her. "I'm guessing you understand that. The feeling of needing space."

She nodded slowly. "I spent four years in a city that never stopped moving. Always noise and people, and there always seemed to be something happening. I thought I'd love it. The energy and the sense of being part of something bigger."

"But you didn't?"

"I felt like I was drowning." The admission surprised her. She hadn't said that out loud to anyone, not even her father. "Every weekend I'd come home, and it was like I could finally breathe again. But then I'd go back to school, and within hours I'd feel that pressure building again. Like the city was crushing me."

"So, why did you apply for jobs there?"

She looked down at her sandwich. "Because I'm supposed to want that, aren't I? The career, the city life, the opportunities. Everyone talks about small-town kids making it big, getting out, doing more. Here I am, the opposite, running back to the small town."

"That's not running back," he said quietly. "That's knowing where you belong."

"But what if I don't belong anywhere? What if I'm too...I don't know, too restless for Timber Ridge but too homesick for anywhere else?"

He was quiet for a moment, and when he spoke, his voice was gentle. "Can I tell you something? About why I moved here?"

She nodded, holding her breath.

"I spent years in Denver, working construction, thinking I had to be in the city to have a real career. To matter. I dated someone..." He paused, seeming to choose his words carefully. "I thought that relationship was what I needed to feel complete. When it ended badly, I was devastated. But more than that, I realized I'd been living someone else's idea of success."

He turned to face her fully. "So, I left. Came to Timber Ridge because it was small and quiet and as far from my old life as I could get while staying in the state. You know what? It was the best decision I ever made."

"Because of the house?"

"Because of the peace. The space to figure out who I actually was, not who I thought I should be." His expression was earnest. "You're not restless, Aleece. You're just trying to figure out where you fit. That's not a weakness. That's being honest."

She felt something loosen in her chest. "How did you know that Timber Ridge was right for you?"

"I felt settled here. Grounded. Like I could finally stop running and just be." He smiled slightly. "Plus, I bought eight acres and a disaster of a house. That definitely committed me to staying."

They both laughed, and the tension eased.

"Eat up." He smirked. "Still got a lot of work ahead of us."

"Like what?" she asked before taking a bite of her sandwich.

"Next, we'll cut and stall the frame that will sit atop the post we just set."

He polished off the rest of his sandwich before rising and heading over to the sawhorses he'd set up earlier.

The work was different now, more precise, requiring careful measuring and cutting. Charles showed her how to use the circular saw, standing behind her to guide her hands, and she tried very hard to focus on the blade and not on his proximity, the warmth of him, the way his voice rumbled near her ear as he explained the technique.

"You're a natural at this," he said after she made her third perfect cut.

"I'm following instructions."

"That's more than most people can manage. Trust me." He smiled at her, and her heart did a stupid little flip. "You actually listen, and you don't try to rush. Those are the two most important things in construction."

They fell into an easy rhythm. With Charles measuring and marking, while she cut. Both of them worked together to secure the boards. The afternoon passed quickly, filled with conversation that flowed naturally from one topic to the next.

Gradually, she realized something: she was happy. Not thinking about job applications or her uncertain future or where she belonged. Just focused on the present moment. Work, conversation, and easy companionship of building something with someone who understood the value of doing it right.

"Okay." He set down the hammer as the sun was starting to sink low in the sky. "That's enough for tonight."

The frame was mostly complete, the deck's structure visible now in the skeletal outline of posts and beams.

"We made good progress," he said, surveying their work with satisfaction. "Better than I expected for one day."

"It's amazing." She stood back, seeing how the deck would flow from the house, how it would frame the view. "I can see what it's going to look like now."

"Can you?" He moved to stand beside her, and together they looked at the emerging structure. "The furniture here, maybe some planters with flowers, string lights overhead. A table where you could eat dinner and watch the sunset."

"You've really envisioned the whole thing."

"Every detail." His voice was soft, almost reverent. "I want it to be perfect."

"For whoever needs it," she said again, that phrase that kept coming up.

He turned to look at her, and the expression on his face was so intense it took her breath away. "Yeah," he said quietly. "For whoever needs it."

They stood there, close enough that she could feel the warmth radiating from him despite the cooling evening air. The moment stretched, heavy with possibility.

"You must be starving," he said abruptly, stepping back. "I've got stuff for dinner if you want to stay. It's the least I can do after you worked all day."

She should probably go home. It was getting late, and she'd already spent the entire day here. But she found herself nodding. "That would be nice."

"It's not much. But I figured a bowl of soup would be perfect after a long day." He led the way inside to the makeshift kitchen, which consisted of a hot plate, a mini fridge, and a camping stove set up on a piece of plywood stretched across two sawhorses. But he moved around it with the same competence he brought to everything else, heating up a pot of chili he'd made earlier and pulling out a loaf of crusty bread.

"Sorry, it's not fancy," he said, ladling chili into mismatched bowls. "Kitchen's not exactly functional yet."

"Are you kidding? This is perfect." It was. Sitting on upturned buckets in the unfinished house, eating simple food while the last light painted everything gold.

They ate in comfortable silence at first, both too hungry to talk. But gradually, the conversation picked up again. Easier now, without the guard that had been there before.

"Thank you for helping today," he said, wiping his bowl with bread. "I didn't realize how much I needed the company until I had it."

"I loved it. Every minute." She met his eyes across the makeshift table. "I can't remember the last time I felt this...useful. Like I was actually doing something that mattered."

"Building matters. Creating things that last." His gaze held hers. "You were good at it. Really good. If you ever decide business isn't for you, you've got a future in construction."

She laughed. "I don't think one day of deck building qualifies me for a career change."

"Maybe not. But you should think about what draws you and what makes you feel like you did today. Useful, engaged, and present." He paused. "That's how you figure out where you belong. Not by logic or practicality, but by paying attention to what makes you feel alive."

The words hung in the air between them, weighted with meaning. She realized she'd been feeling alive all day, even with her muscles aching and her hands dirty. Working beside him, learning from him, being trusted to help build something beautiful. Was it the work that made her feel this way? Or was it him?

"I should probably head home," she said, even though every part of her wanted to stay. "Dad will wonder where I am."

"Right, of course." He stood quickly, gathering their bowls. "Let me walk you out."

They moved through the darkening house to the front door. Outside, the temperature had dropped significantly, and her breath fogged in the cold air. Stars were starting to appear overhead, brilliant against the darkening sky.

"Thank you for letting me help," she said as they reached her car. "For teaching me and sharing this with me."

"Thank you for coming and seeing what this place could be." His voice was rough. "It means more than you know."

They stood in the driveway, neither quite willing to say goodbye. The space between them felt charged, electric, like the air before a storm.

She found herself stepping closer. "Charles—"

He moved too, closing the distance until they were inches apart. His hand came up, almost touching her face, and her breath caught. This was it. He was going to kiss her, and everything would be perfect.

His hand fell away, and he stepped back abruptly, something like

69

pain crossing his face. "You should go. It's getting late, and the roads can be tricky in the dark."

The rejection stung, sharp and unexpected. "Oh, okay."

"Aleece..." He reached for her again, then stopped himself. "I'll see you...when will I see you?"

"I don't know. When do you need help again?"

"Whenever you want to come back. Tomorrow? Next week? Just come back."

There was something desperate in his voice that eased some of the hurt. "Tomorrow, if that's okay."

"That's more than okay." His expression softened, and for a moment, he looked so hopeful and vulnerable that her heart ached. "Tomorrow. Same time?"

"I'll be here."

She got in her car, and he stood watching as she started the engine. In her rearview mirror, she could see him still standing there as she drove away, a solitary figure outlined against the light from the house.

The drive home passed in a blur. Her mind replayed the almost-kiss repeatedly. The way he'd looked at her before he'd stepped back. The conflict was clear on his face. He wanted to close the distance but forced himself not to. Why? What was stopping him?

When she arrived home, her father was in the living room, and one look at her face made him set his book down.

"How was the deck building?" he asked.

"Good. We got a lot done." She collapsed onto the sofa, exhausted in every way. "I'm going back tomorrow."

"Are you?" His lips curled up into a knowing smile.

"Don't start."

"I didn't say anything."

"I can see you thinking things." She shook her head.

Her father continued to smile at her. "I'm thinking you look happy. Happier than you've been since you got home. That's all I'm thinking."

She wanted to argue, but she couldn't, because he was right. Today, working beside Charles, learning from him, being trusted with something that mattered so much to him, she'd been happy. More than happy. She'd felt like she belonged.

But Charles had pulled away. Had stopped himself from kissing her and had looked at her like she was something he wanted but couldn't let himself have.

"It's complicated," she said finally.

"The best things usually are." Her father stood, patting her shoulder as he passed. "Get some rest. You're going to be sore tomorrow."

As he headed toward the kitchen, she went to her. She quickly showered and changed, her muscles already beginning to protest the day's work. But despite the physical exhaustion, her mind wouldn't settle.

Not wanting to face her father's knowing gaze, she curled up in bed. She stared at the ceiling, replaying every moment. The patience in his voice when he explained techniques, or the careful way he'd stood behind her at the saw, close but not too close. The intensity in his eyes when he'd talked about the house being perfect for "whoever needs it." And that moment in the driveway. The almost-kiss that he'd stopped at the last second, looking like it cost him everything to pull away.

Why did he keep doing that? Why did he look at her like she was everything he wanted but refused to let himself touch her?

She rolled onto her side, looking out her window at the stars. Somewhere out there, Charles was probably still at his house, working on something or lying on his air mattress in that beautiful, finished bedroom, staring at the same stars. Was he thinking about her?

Tomorrow. I'll see him tomorrow.

The thought sent a flutter through her chest. Excitement, nervousness, and something deeper that she wasn't quite ready to name.

One day of building a deck, and she was already counting the hours until she could go back.

This was more than an attraction or a crush. This was something that pulled at her, fundamental and undeniable. And whether Charles wanted to admit it or not, she was pretty sure he felt it too. She just had to figure out what was stopping him from acting on it and whether she was brave enough to push past whatever walls he'd built around himself.

CHAPTER 7
FALLING INTO RHYTHM

For three weeks, Aleece had been helping Charles at the house. It had become the center of her world in a way she hadn't anticipated. They'd fallen into a schedule of working on the house every Tuesday, Thursday, and Saturday. Sometimes she stayed for a few hours, other times she was there the entire day. It depended on what he was working on, what he needed help with, and how much her body could take after days of physical labor she wasn't used to.

The deck was nearly finished now. They'd laid all the boards, sanded everything smooth, and applied the first coat of stain. It was beautiful. Exactly as Charles had envisioned it, flowing seamlessly from the house and framing the view perfectly.

But they'd moved on to other projects, too. He had started on the kitchen cabinets, which were custom-built from reclaimed wood. She helped with sanding, holding pieces steady while he assembled them, and applying finish in thin, careful coats.

"You're getting good at this," he said one afternoon, examining her work on a cabinet door. "Look at that. No drips, even coverage, and smooth as glass."

She tried not to glow at the praise. "I had a good teacher."

"You're a good student. Makes a difference." He set the door aside to dry and pulled out the next one. "Most people rush. They want to be done, so they slap on too much finish and end up with runs and drips. But you take your time. Do it right."

"Because you'd make me sand it down and start over if I didn't," she teased.

"Damn right I would." But he was smiling as he said it. That rare, full smile that transformed his whole face and made her heart skip.

She'd learned a lot about him over these weeks. Small things, gleaned from casual conversation and careful observation.

He drank his coffee black and could go through an entire pot by himself in a day. There was a scar on his left shoulder from a construction accident years ago. Even though he was left-handed, he taught himself to use tools with his right hand, too, for better leverage. He hummed while he worked, nothing recognizable, just a low, tuneless sound that meant he was focused and content.

He was patient to a fault when teaching her something new, but had no tolerance for sloppy work. He'd make her redo something three times if it wasn't right, but he'd never make her feel bad about it. Just explain what was wrong and show her how to fix it.

Perhaps one of her favorite things about it was that he was funny. Not in an obvious way, but with a dry wit that caught her off guard and made her laugh until her sides hurt.

On Saturday, when a board didn't fit right, and she'd spent ten minutes trying to force it into place, before he gently took it from her.

"The thing about wood," he'd said solemnly, "is that it doesn't respond well to threats and violence. You have to sweet-talk it."

"Sweet-talk it?" She cocked an eyebrow at him.

"Absolutely. Tell it how pretty it is. Promise it a good finish. Maybe some polyurethane if it behaves."

She'd dissolved into giggles, and he'd grinned at her, clearly pleased with himself.

But it wasn't just the work or the humor or even the teaching that drew her back three times a week. It was Charles himself. She loved watching him work. The way his large hands moved with such precision and care. How he'd frown slightly when measuring, double and triple-checking before making a cut. The way he'd step back to assess something, arms crossed, head tilted, completely absorbed.

She loved the quiet competence he brought to everything. How he never seemed rushed or stressed, just methodical and focused. He anticipated problems before they happened and had solutions ready. There was also the way he treated every piece of wood, every joint, every detail as if it mattered.

She loved the way he was with her. Patient and kind, trusting her with important tasks, teaching her not by lecturing but by showing and then letting her try. The way he'd correct her mistakes without making her feel stupid, and how he'd praise her successes like they were genuine achievements.

Increasingly, she found herself watching him when she should have been working. Admiring the play of muscles in his forearms as he gripped a board. The concentration on his face when he was measuring. Or the satisfaction in his expression when something came together perfectly.

Sometimes she'd even catch him watching her, too. It would happen when she was focused on sanding or painting, when she thought he was absorbed in his own work. She'd look up and find his gaze on her, dark and intense, with an expression that made her breath catch. Then he'd quickly look away, busying himself with whatever was nearest.

There were moments when she thought something would happen, when the air between them felt charged, electric, and full of possibility.

Like last Thursday, when they'd been working on installing the kitchen cabinets. The space was tight, and they'd both been reaching for the same tool. Their hands had collided, and his fingers had wrapped around hers for just a second. The touch had sent electricity up her arm, and she'd looked up to find him staring at their joined hands with an expression of such longing it had made her heart ache. Then he'd released her and stepped back, creating distance.

Earlier, when she'd been on a ladder installing the last pieces of crown molding in the master bedroom. She'd lost her balance slightly, and Charles had been there instantly, hands on her waist, steadying her. She'd looked down at him and seen everything she was feeling reflected in his eyes.

For a heartbeat, neither of them had moved. His hands had been warm through her shirt, and she'd been very aware of how easy it would be to lean down, to close the small distance between them. But then he'd cleared his throat and stepped away, holding the ladder steady while she climbed down, his expression carefully neutral.

It was maddening. Every instinct told her Charles felt the same pull she did. The way he looked at her, the way he unconsciously leaned toward her when they talked, or how his voice softened when he said her name. The tension crackled between them whenever they were close. But he never acted on it. Never crossed that invisible line or even acknowledged what was happening between them.

It was to the point she was starting to doubt herself. Was she imagining it? Maybe the attraction was one-sided, and she was just seeing what she wanted to see. Maybe Charles was just being kind to a lonely woman who'd latched onto him for no good reason. That very idea made her chest tight with humiliation.

But then she'd catch him watching her again, or he'd smile at something she said, or his hand would linger a moment too long when passing her a tool, and she was certain he felt it too. So why wouldn't he do anything about it?

Tuesday evening, Aleece arrived home later than usual because they'd finished the kitchen cabinet installation. She was exhausted, covered in sawdust, and probably had wood stain under her fingernails despite wearing gloves.

As she entered the kitchen, her father looked up from his dinner. "Long day at the office?"

"Ha ha." She dropped her bag and collapsed into a chair. "We got all the lower cabinets installed. They look amazing, Dad. You should see them."

"I'm sure they do. Charles does good work." He stood and grabbed a plate from the microwave. He'd saved her some meatloaf and mashed potatoes. "You've been spending a lot of time out there."

"There's a lot of work to do."

"Mm-hmm." Her father sat down and took a bite, chewing thoughtfully. "And how's Charles doing?"

"Fine. Why?"

"Just wondering. You two seem to be getting along well."

She felt heat creep up her neck. "We work well together. That's all."

"That's all?" He raised an eyebrow. "Sweetheart, you've been going to that house three times a week for almost a month. You talk about Charles constantly, and you light up every time you mention something you worked on together. When you come home, you look happier than I've seen you since you got back from college."

"I like the work. It's satisfying. Makes me feel useful."

"I'm sure the work is satisfying." His tone was gentle. "But I don't think that's the only reason you're going back."

She pushed potatoes around her plate. "What do you want me to say?"

"I want you to be honest. With yourself, at least." He set down his fork. "Do you have feelings for Charles?"

The direct question made her squirm. "I don't know. Maybe. It's complicated."

"Why is it complicated?"

"Because we've known each other for less than a month, and I don't even know if he..." She stopped, frustrated.

"If he what? Feels the same way?"

"Yeah." Her voice was small. "Sometimes I think he does. The way he looks at me or how he is when we're working together, but then he pulls away. Like he's stopping himself from getting too close. I don't know if that means he's not interested or if there's something else going on."

He was quiet for a moment. "Have you asked him?"

"What? No! I can't just ask him if he has feelings for me. That's ridiculous."

"Why is it ridiculous? You're both adults. If there's something between you, talking about it seems like the logical next step."

"What if I'm wrong?" Her voice rose slightly. "What if I've been reading everything wrong and I make a fool of myself? Or worse, what if I'm right, but he's not interested for some reason, and asking makes everything awkward, and I can't go back to the house anymore?"

The thought of not being able to go back and not seeing Charles made something twist painfully in her chest.

"Aleece." Her father reached across the table, covering her hand with his. "I've known Charles for years. He's a good man, but he keeps to himself. Doesn't let people in easily. If he's letting you in, letting you be part of his house, his project, his space, that means something."

"But what if it just means he needs help with construction?"

"Honey, Charles has been working on that house alone for over a year. If all he needed was help, he could have hired someone. The fact that he's letting you work with him, teaching you, sharing that space with you, that's not just about needing an extra pair of hands." He squeezed her hand.

She wanted to believe him. But doubt gnawed at her. "Then why does he pull away? Every time I think something might happen, he backs off."

"I don't know. But that's something you should ask him, not me."

"I can't."

"Why not?"

"I'm scared." The admission felt raw. "I'm scared that if I push, he'll pull away completely. I'd rather have what we have now, even if it's just friendship and working together, than lose him entirely."

Her father's expression softened with understanding. "I get that. I do. But sweetheart, living in that uncertainty, always wondering, that's its own kind of pain. Sometimes you have to take the risk."

Deep down, she knew he was right, but knowing something logically and having the courage to act on it were two different things.

They finished eating in silence. It was as if he understood she needed time to process what he'd said. Even after dinner, while she showered and got ready for bed, his words stayed with her. No matter how scared she was, she knew she had to take the risk. Otherwise, she'd always wonder.

By Thursday morning, when Aleece arrived at the house, she wasn't sure she was brave enough to address the situation between them. She wanted answers, but she wasn't sure she was ready for the cost that may come with them.

She entered the kitchen to find Charles already at work. The cabinets they'd installed looked incredible. The wood glowed warm in the morning light, every joint perfect, every line clean.

"Morning," Charles said, looking over at her with that soft smile that always made her heart skip. "Ready to start on the uppers?"

"Ready."

They fell into their familiar rhythm. He measured and marked, while she helped position the heavy cabinets, and they worked together to secure them to the wall. It required coordination and trust, and they'd gotten good at anticipating each other's movements.

"Little to the left," he said, holding the level against the cabinet. "Perfect. Hold it there."

She braced the cabinet, her arms already protesting, while he secured the first screws. They were standing close, and she could feel the heat of him, smell sawdust, soap, and something uniquely him.

"You okay?" he asked, glancing at her. "Need a break?"

"I'm good."

But she wasn't. Being this close to him, working in sync with him, feeling the brush of his arm against hers, it was overwhelming. The pull she felt toward him seemed to be getting stronger instead of fading, and maintaining the careful distance between them was becoming harder.

"There." He stepped back, admiring their work. "That's the first one. Only five more to go."

"Only five?" She groaned dramatically, and he laughed.

"Come on. I'll buy you lunch when we're done."

They worked through the morning, installing cabinet after cabinet. The conversation flowed easily. They laughed, teased each other, and fell into comfortable silences. But underneath it all, she felt the tension. The awareness of the unspoken thing between them seemed to grow heavier with each passing day.

Until finally it came to a head as they installed the last cabinet. The tricky one over the sink that had to be precisely positioned. Both were on ladders, working from opposite sides, as he walked her through the measurements.

"Just a quarter inch higher on your side," he said, watching the level. "There. Perfect."

They secured the cabinet together, and when it was done, they both paused. She was on one ladder, he was on the other, the cabinet between them, looking at what they'd accomplished.

"We did it," she said softly.

"Yeah." His voice was rough. "We make a good team."

Their gazes met, and something in his expression made her breath catch. He was looking at her as if she were precious and important. Like she mattered in a way that went beyond helping with renovations.

"Charles—" she started.

"Lunch," he said abruptly, breaking eye contact and climbing down from his ladder. "I promised you lunch. There's this place in town that makes great sandwiches. We could go, if you want. Or I could pick something up and bring it back. Whatever you prefer."

The moment was gone, and she felt the frustration rise in her chest. This was what he always did. Pulled away right when she thought they might finally address what was happening between them.

She climbed down from her ladder slowly, trying to find the courage her father had talked about. The courage to ask and take the risk.

"Charles." Her voice came out steadier than she felt. "Can I ask you something?"

He turned to face her, and she saw wariness flicker across his expression. "Sure."

"Why do you do that?"

"Do what?"

"Pull away. Every time there's a moment between us, every time I think..." She stopped for a moment before she forced herself to continue. "You feel it too, don't you? This...whatever this is between us?"

He went very still. "Aleece—"

"I'm not imagining it. I know I'm not. The way you look at me sometimes, the way you..." She gestured helplessly, unsure how to put it into words. "But then you pull back. I need to know if it's because you're not interested, or if there's something else. I can't keep wondering."

The silence stretched between them, heavy and charged. His jaw clenched, and she saw him fighting some internal battle.

"I feel it," he finally said, his voice low. "Of course I feel it."

Her heart leaped. "Then why do you keep pulling away?"

"It's complicated." He ran a hand through his hair, frustration clear on his face. "You don't understand. There are things about me, about shifters...it's just not that simple."

"Then explain it to me. Make me understand."

"I can't. Not yet. I need..." He shook his head. "I'm sorry. I know that's not fair to you."

She felt tears prick her eyes, and she blinked them back angrily. "You're right, it's not fair. I've been coming here for weeks, spending time with you, feeling this connection, and you won't even tell me why we can't act on it?"

"It's not about want." He took a step toward her, then stopped himself. "Believe me, Aleece. It's not about want."

"Then what is it about?"

But he just shook his head. "I need time. To figure things out. To make sure—" He stopped again, seeming to struggle with something. "Just...give me a little more time. Please."

She wanted to push harder, to demand answers. But as she looked into her eyes, she could see the pain, and she stopped.

"Okay," she said quietly. "But Charles, I can't do this indefinitely. The not knowing. The tension. Eventually, something has to give."

"I know." His voice was barely above a whisper. "I know."

They stood in the unfinished kitchen, surrounded by the beautiful cabinets they'd installed together, and the distance between them felt wider than ever despite being only a few feet apart.

"I should go." She grabbed her bag. "I'll see you Saturday?"

"If you still want to come."

"I want to come." Despite everything, despite the frustration and confusion, she still wanted to be here with him. "I just need honesty, Charles. Whatever this is, whatever the complication is, I need you to eventually tell me."

"I will." He looked at her with such intensity that it made her ache. "I promise. Soon."

She left without another word, climbing into her car with shaking hands. In her rearview mirror, she could see Charles standing in the doorway of his house, watching her leave.

She drove home in a daze, replaying the conversation. He felt it too. He'd admitted that much. But there was a complication that kept him from acting on it. She didn't understand what it could be. What would make someone pull away from a connection this strong?

When she arrived home, she found her father in the living room with a file of papers in his lap. He looked up and instantly set the papers aside.

"What happened?"

"I asked him." She collapsed onto the sofa. "I asked if he felt it too."

"And?"

"He said yes. But he won't tell me why we can't do anything about it. Says it's complicated. That he needs time." She looked at her father. "What does that mean? What could be so complicated?"

Her father was quiet for a long moment. "Did he say anything about being a shifter?"

"He mentioned it. Said there were things about shifters I didn't understand." She frowned. "But what does that have to do with anything? Plenty of shifters date humans. You raised me. I'm human, and it was fine."

"It was," he agreed carefully. "But there are aspects of shifter culture and biology that can complicate relationships. Especially certain kinds of relationships."

"What are you talking about?"

But her father shook his head. "It's not my place to explain. If Charles has something to tell you, he needs to be the one to do it. I'm just saying that you should be patient with him. Whatever he's working through, I'm sure he has good reasons."

She wanted to scream with frustration. Everyone kept talking in riddles, hinting at complications without explaining what they were. But she thought about the look on Charles' face when he told her it wasn't about want. The pain was there in his words. Whatever was holding him back, it wasn't simple. Instead, it was clearly tearing him apart.

"Okay," she said finally. "I'll wait, but not forever."

"That's fair," her father said. "And Aleece? Whatever happens, I'm proud of you for being brave enough to ask."

She lay there on the sofa as her thoughts circled back to Charles' face as he stood in the kitchen.

I feel it. Of course, I feel it.

There are things about me, about shifters, that you don't understand.

What things? What could be so complicated that it would keep two people who clearly cared about each other apart?

Saturday felt very far away. Two days of not seeing Charles, of wondering and waiting and trying to be patient when every instinct screamed at her to go back to that house and demand answers. But she'd given her word. She'd wait. She just hoped that whatever he needed to figure out, he'd do it soon. Because this limbo was becoming unbearable, and Aleece wasn't sure how much longer her heart could take it.

CHAPTER 8
THE ALMOST CONFESSION

Saturday came, and despite the awkwardness of Thursday's conversation, Aleece found herself driving to Charles' house exactly on time. She'd thought about not going and giving them both space, but the pull was too strong, and besides, she'd told him she'd be there.

When she arrived, she found Charles' truck in the driveway and could hear sounds of work coming from inside the house. She got out of her car and stood there for a moment, looking up at the house that was coming together. One day, it wouldn't just be a house, it would be a home. The thought of Charles there with someone else sent a pang of longing through her. Brushing it aside, she forced herself to go inside. It didn't take long before she found him upstairs in one of the guest bedrooms, the larger one at the front of the house.

"Hey," he said, looking up from where he was prying up old baseboards. There was a wariness in his eyes, like he wasn't sure what to expect after Thursday.

"Hi." She set down her bag. "What are we working on today?"

Relief flickered across his face. "This room. Finally ready to finish it. Floors are next, then paint, then trim." He gestured around the space. "Thought we could start with the floor prep. Pulling up the old tack strips, checking for damage."

"Sounds good."

They fell into work, and gradually the tension eased. Not completely, there was still that awareness between them, that unspoken thing that charged the air. But the comfortable rhythm they'd developed over the past weeks returned, and she found herself relaxing.

The guest bedroom was beautiful, or would be once it was finished. It was almost as large as the master, with big windows that looked out over the front of the property, including the driveway winding through the trees and the forest beyond. Morning light poured in, warm and golden, making even the damaged floors and bare walls look promising.

"This is going to be a gorgeous room," she said, pausing to look out the windows. "The light is incredible."

"That's why I'm doing this one next. After the master, it's got the best natural light." He came to stand beside her, following her gaze. "Figured whoever stayed here should have a nice view to wake up to."

"Who do you imagine staying here? Future guests?"

He was quiet for a moment. "Maybe. Or..." He trailed off, seeming to reconsider his words. "Just nice to have the space ready, for whatever comes."

There it was again. That vague reference to the future, to whoever might need these spaces. She studied his profile, trying to understand.

"Charles," she said carefully, "can I ask you something personal?"

He turned to look at her, the wariness back in his eyes. "Okay."

"Why haven't you settled down? Gotten married, had a family?" She saw him tense. "I'm not trying to pry. You've built this beautiful home, put so much work into making it perfect. It seems like the kind of house meant for a family. But you talk about it like you're waiting for something."

He stepped back from the window and crouched down to examine a section of the floor. But she could see the tension in his shoulders, the way his hands stilled on the wood.

"I've been waiting for the right person," he finally said, his voice low.

"For a long time?"

"It feels like for my whole life." He looked up at her then. She could see the longing and pain in his deep brown eyes. "Some people know exactly what they want, exactly who they're looking for. They can picture them clearly, imagine every detail of the life they'll build together."

"Is that how it is for you?"

"Yeah." His gaze held hers. "I know exactly who I'm waiting for. I've known for a while now."

The air between them felt thick, charged. Her heart was pounding. "Does she know? The person you're waiting for?"

His jaw clenched. "I'm trying to tell her. Trying to do it right."

"Why is it so hard? If you know who she is, if you're building all this for her." She gestured to the house around them. "Why wait?"

"Because I want her to have a choice." The words came out raw, pained. "I want her to choose me because she wants to, not because of other reasons. Not because she feels obligated or bound by something she doesn't fully understand yet."

She wanted to push further, to ask what that meant, what reasons or obligations he was talking about, but there was a vulnerability in his eyes that looked like it was costing him everything to show her. Instead, she moved closer, sitting on the floor beside where he crouched. "Can I tell you something? About me?"

He nodded, and some of the tension in his shoulders eased slightly.

"I'm scared," she whispered. "Scared of ending up like my mother."

"What do you mean?"

"My biological mother gave me up when I was just a baby. Left me in Timber Ridge in the middle of winter, in January, with just a note." She picked at a loose thread on her jeans. "Growing up, I used to have these nightmares. That I'd be somewhere, sometimes I was at school, other times I was at a friend's house, and when I turned around, everyone would be gone. Like I'd been left behind again."

"Aleece—" His voice was soft.

"I used to wake up crying, and Dad would come sit with me until I fell back asleep. But the fear never really went away that I'm somehow...fundamentally unwanted. That there's something wrong with me that made my own mother leave me in the cold." She felt tears prick her eyes and blinked them back. "Dad tried to tell me it wasn't about me, that my mother must have had her reasons. But when you're a kid, you don't understand that. You just know you weren't enough to make her stay."

"That's not true." Charles moved to sit fully on the floor beside her, close enough that their shoulders almost touched. "What your mother did wasn't about you being unwanted. It was about her circumstances and her choices. Nothing about you."

"How can you know that?"

"Because I see you." He turned to face her fully. "I see how hard you work, the patience you have when you're learning something new, and how you light up when you understand a new concept. I see how kind you are, that you care about doing things right, and that you've thrown yourself into helping with this house even though you had no obligation to." His voice dropped lower. "I see you, Aleece, and there's nothing unwanted about you. *Nothing*."

The tears came then, slipping down her cheeks before she could stop them. "Then why did she leave me? Why would someone give up their child if there wasn't something wrong?"

"I don't know." He reached up, gently wiping away a tear with his thumb. The touch was soft, careful, as if she were something precious that might break. "But I know it wasn't because you weren't enough. You're more than enough."

She looked at him and at the tenderness in his eyes, the certainty in his expression, the way he was touching her face like it was the most natural thing in the world. "How can you be so sure?"

"Because—" He stopped and seemed to struggle with something internal. "Because anyone who really saw you, who really knew you, would know how rare you are. How special."

"Charles—"

"I'm sorry." He dropped his hand and started to pull back. "I shouldn't have…"

She caught his hand, holding it against her cheek. "Don't pull away. Not this time."

They stared at each other, frozen in the moment. His hand was warm against her face, and she leaned into it slightly, letting herself have this small contact.

"I don't understand what's happening between us," she said quietly. "I know it's real, and you feel it too. I'm tired of pretending I don't."

"Aleece, if you knew…" Charles' voice was rough. "There are things about me, about what I am, that complicate this."

"Then tell me. Help me understand."

"I want to. I truly want to." His thumb moved slightly, caressing her cheekbone, and her breath hitched. "But I need you to know what you're choosing. I need you to understand everything before…"

"Before what?"

His gaze dropped to her lips, and she saw the moment he decided. He leaned in slowly, giving her time to pull away, and she didn't. She wouldn't. She'd been waiting for this for weeks.

Their lips were inches apart when his phone rang, shrill and insistent in the quiet room.

They froze. He closed his eyes, jaw clenching with frustration. "I'm sorry. I have to. It might be a client emergency."

He leaned back and pulled out his phone. Instantly, she felt the loss of his warmth like a physical ache. Her attention focused on him as he checked the screen and saw his expression shift to concern.

"It's the Andersons." He looked at her apologetically. "The other day their furnace started acting up, so I need to take this."

"Of course."

He stood, taking the call as he walked toward the door. "Hey, Mrs. Anderson. What's going on?"

Aleece sat on the floor, heart pounding, trying to process what had almost just happened. He'd almost kissed her. Finally, after weeks of tension and pulling away, he'd almost closed that distance. It had felt right. Natural. Like something that had been building toward this moment all along.

She touched her face where his hand had been, still feeling the warmth of his skin against hers.

Charles returned a few minutes later, looking frustrated. "I'm sorry. I need to go. Their furnace is completely out, and it's supposed to drop below freezing tonight. They have a baby...I can't leave them without heat."

"I understand." She stood, brushing off her jeans. "Of course you need to go."

"I'm sorry. I..." Charles ran a hand through his hair. "Can we talk? Later? Maybe tomorrow?"

"Tomorrow's Sunday. You don't usually work on Sundays."

"I could make an exception. If you wanted to come by." He looked at her, hope burning with intensity in his gaze. "I think we need to talk. Really talk about everything."

"Okay." Her voice came out steadier than she felt. "Tomorrow. What time?"

"Noon? I'll make lunch."

"Noon," she agreed.

They stood in the guest bedroom, surrounded by half-finished renovation work, and the moment felt weighted with significance. Whatever conversation they were going to have tomorrow would change things. She could feel it.

"I should let you go," she said. "The Andersons need you."

"Yeah." But he didn't move, just looked at her like he was memorizing her face. "Aleece?"

"Yeah?"

"What I said before about you being more than enough? I meant that. Whatever your mother's reasons were for leaving you, it wasn't because you weren't worth staying for."

Fresh tears pricked her eyes. "Thank you for saying that."

"It's the truth." He took a step toward her, then stopped himself. "I'll see you tomorrow. We'll talk, and I'll explain everything. I promise."

"Okay."

He left, his footsteps heavy on the stairs, and moments later, she heard his truck start up and pull away. She stood in the empty guest bedroom, touching her face again where he'd touched her, replaying every word of their conversation.

I know exactly who I'm waiting for. I've known for a while now.

Was he talking about her? It seemed like he was. The way he'd looked at her when he said it, the tenderness in his voice when he'd wiped away her tears. But what was he waiting for? What did he need to tell her that was so complicated?

She walked through the house slowly, seeing it with new eyes. Every room Charles had finished, every detail he'd perfected. Was he doing it for her? Building this home with her in mind? The idea of it made her heart race with hope and fear in equal measure.

In the master bedroom, she stood at the window looking out at the view. She could imagine waking up here, seeing this every morning. Coming home to this house, this space that he had built with such care.

More importantly, coming home to Charles. The image was so vivid, so right, that it took her breath away.

But there was still tomorrow. Still, whatever conversation he needed to have, whatever he needed to explain.

As Aleece pulled into the driveway at home, she spotted her father in the garden. Despite the cold, he was preparing the garden beds for spring planting. She shut off her car, got out, and strolled toward him.

"You're home early," he commented, looking up from turning soil.

"Charles had an emergency. The Andersons' furnace."

"Ah. Poor timing."

"Yeah." She sat on the porch steps, watching him work. "Dad? Can I ask you something about my biological mother?"

Her father set down his spade and came to sit beside her. "Of course."

"Do you know anything about why she left me? I mean, really? Beyond what's in the note?"

He was quiet for a moment. "I've told you everything I know from the official records, but I've always suspected there was more to the story."

"Like what?"

"Like the fact that she left you in the warmest, safest place in town. She left you on the fire station steps, where she knew you'd be found immediately. Like the note that said, 'Please take care of her.' Not 'I don't want her' but 'take care of her.' She made sure you had a blanket and were bundled warm, even though it was January." Her father put his arm around her shoulders. "That doesn't sound like a mother who didn't want you. It sounds like a mother who loved you enough to make an impossible choice."

"But why? What choice?"

"I don't know, sweetheart. I wish I did." He squeezed her shoulder. "But I've always believed your mother loved you. Whatever drove her to leave you, I don't think it was because you weren't enough."

It was the second time today someone had said those words to her. *You're more than enough.* She leaned into her father's embrace, letting herself be comforted.

"Charles said something similar," she admitted.

"Did he?"

"We were talking. About my fears of being unwanted, and he said—" She stopped, emotion clogging her throat. "He said there was nothing unwanted about me. That anyone who really saw me would know how rare I am."

Her father was quiet for a long moment. "He's right, and I'm glad he sees that."

"Dad, I think..." She took a shaky breath. "I think I'm falling for Charles. It scares me because I don't know if he feels the same way. I don't want to be the person who reads too much into things and ends up hurt."

"What does your gut tell you? Does he feel the same way?"

She considered the way Charles looked at her. How he caressed her face and their almost kiss before the phone rang. "Yes. I think he does, but there's something holding him back. Something he says he needs to explain."

"Then listen when he explains, and then decide what you want."

"Tomorrow," she said. "He wants to talk tomorrow."

"Well, then." Her father stood and held out a hand to help her up. "Tomorrow you'll get your answers."

Tomorrow, everything would change. She just had to be brave enough to hear it, and brave enough to choose what came next.

CHAPTER 9
DINNER AT HOME

Aleece woke Sunday morning with nervous energy thrumming through her veins. Charles had said noon, and they'd talk about everything. That left way too much time on her hands. She spent the morning trying to distract herself by cleaning her room, answering emails, and pretending to work on job applications, but her thoughts kept drifting to that moment in the guest bedroom. The way Charles had looked at her as his thumb had moved across her cheekbone. They'd come so close to kissing.

At eleven-thirty, her phone buzzed with a text from Charles.

I'm so sorry. This emergency job is running long. Pipe burst at the community center. Can we reschedule? Tomorrow evening? I could make dinner.

She stared at the message, disappointment warring with understanding. Of course, he had emergencies. That was his job. But the anticipation she'd built up all morning, now deflated like a balloon. Still, she texted back.

Of course. Tomorrow works. Hope the pipe wasn't too bad.

It could have been worse. I'm really sorry about today. Tomorrow, I promise. We'll talk.

She set down her phone and flopped back on her bed, staring at the ceiling. Another day of waiting and not knowing.

She heard her father downstairs in the kitchen. She needed lunch, so she forced herself up off the bed and headed downstairs. When she reached the bottom of the steps, she could see her father pulling ingredients from the refrigerator.

"Making lunch?" she asked.

"Dinner, actually. I invited Charles over." Her father glanced at her. "Is that okay? I know you two were supposed to meet today, but when I heard about the community center emergency, I figured he'd be working late and hungry. Thought I'd save him from another night of takeout."

Her heart lifted despite herself. "He's coming here? For dinner?"

"Around six. Unless that's awkward? I can cancel if you'd rather—"

"No." She moved into the kitchen. "No, that's good. What are you making?"

"Pot roast. Charles mentioned once that he missed home-cooked meals." Her father set vegetables on the counter and glanced toward her. "You could help, if you want. Or make yourself scarce if you need space."

"I'll help." She grabbed a cutting board. "What do you need me to do?"

The idea of Charles coming for dinner meant maybe she'd get some answers before the next day. Maybe they could slip away and talk.

They spent the afternoon cooking together, and Aleece tried not to think about the fact that in a few hours, Charles would be here. In her house. Having dinner with her and her father, like they were a family, or at least more than just the handyman she'd been helping with renovations.

By six o'clock, the house smelled incredible, and she had changed her outfit three times before settling on jeans and a soft blue sweater. Casual but nice. Not like she was trying too hard.

Her father, infuriatingly observant as always, just smiled and said nothing.

Charles' truck pulled into the driveway exactly at six. She watched through the window as he got out, running a hand through his hair. He was wearing jeans and a dark green long-sleeved shirt, and he looked tired and somehow both nervous and hopeful.

Her father went to answer the door before she could move. "Charles! Come in, come in. How was the community center disaster?"

"Could have been worse. Got it patched up, but they'll need new pipes installed next week." Charles stepped inside, and his gaze immediately found her standing in the living room. His expression softened. "Hey."

"Hi." She moved closer. "Rough day?"

"Long day. But better now." The way he said it, the warmth in his gaze made her pulse quicken.

"Well, dinner's ready whenever you are," Thomas said, leading them toward the dining room. "Hope you're hungry. I might have made enough to feed half the town."

The dining room table was set for three, and her father had clearly put effort into making it nice. He used actual cloth napkins, the good dishes, and candles in the center. It felt oddly formal and intimate at once.

They settled in, passing dishes around, and she found herself hyperaware of Charles across the table. The way his large hands handled the serving spoons carefully, and how he thanked Thomas for each dish passed. Under the table, his knee was close enough to hers that she could feel the warmth of him.

"This is incredible," Charles said after his first bite. "Thank you for inviting me. I can't remember the last time I had a home-cooked meal like this."

"Aleece helped," her father praised. "She made the roasted vegetables."

Charles looked at her. "They're perfect."

The conversation flowed easily, surprisingly so. Thomas asked about Charles' work, and Charles asked about Thomas' upcoming town council meeting. They talked about Timber Ridge, about the summer kickoff carnival preparations, and about the Andersons' new grandchild.

But she noticed something she hadn't fully registered before—the way Thomas and Charles interacted. There was a comfort there, a familiarity that suggested they'd been talking more than she'd realized. The way Thomas asked specific questions about the house renovation, and how Charles seemed to understand references to town politics that Aleece didn't follow.

"How long have you two been talking?" she asked during a lull in conversation. "I mean, beyond just around town?"

Thomas and Charles exchanged a look, and she saw something pass between them, something that was edged with understanding and conspiracy.

"We have coffee sometimes," her father admitted. "When Charles is in town for supplies. I've been following the progress on his house."

"You have?"

"Of course. It's an impressive project." Her father took a sip of wine. "Plus, Charles here has been a good sounding board for some town council issues. He's got good instincts for construction and development."

Charles looked slightly uncomfortable with the praise. "I just offer opinions when asked."

"Good opinions," her father insisted. "You helped us avoid a major mistake with the new park pavilion design."

She looked between them, realizing there was a relationship here she hadn't fully understood. Thomas and Charles weren't just acquaintances. They'd developed a friendship built on mutual respect and apparently regular coffee meetings.

"You never mentioned that," she said to her father.

"You never asked." But he was smiling.

As dinner progressed, Thomas began telling stories about Aleece's childhood. Embarrassing ones like her first day of kindergarten when she'd insisted on wearing a princess costume, and the time she'd tried to build a treehouse and ended up stuck on the roof. When he started with her disastrous attempt at learning to drive, she cut him off.

"Dad," she protested, her face heating. "Charles doesn't need to hear about me crashing into the mailbox."

"It was barely a dent," her father said, eyes twinkling. "And you were only sixteen. Everyone has a rough start."

"I backed into a telephone pole my first week driving," Charles offered, and she shot him a grateful look. "Twice. Same pole."

Thomas laughed. "Well, at least Aleece only hit the mailbox once."

Despite the embarrassment, she found herself enjoying it. The way Charles listened to each story with genuine interest, smiling at her childhood antics, and the way her father clearly enjoyed sharing these moments, as if he were presenting pieces of Aleece's history for Charles to know and understand.

It felt like Charles was being brought into the family. Like her father was giving his approval and his blessing in the form of shared stories and comfortable dinner conversation.

After they'd eaten their fill and helped clean up, her father turned toward them. "I have to run to the office."

"Now?" She looked at the clock. It was nearly eight.

"I forgot some paperwork I need for tomorrow's meeting. Won't take long." Her father was already grabbing his keys. "You two should enjoy the porch. It's actually nice out for January."

He was gone before she could protest, and she was left standing in the kitchen with Charles, very aware they were suddenly alone. It wasn't the first time, but there was a tension in the air because of the pending conversation.

"The porch sounds nice," Charles said quietly. "If you want?"

"Yeah. Okay."

They grabbed jackets and moved outside. The porch swing creaked slightly as they sat, not quite touching but close enough that she could feel the warmth of him beside her. The evening was unusually mild, and stars were beginning to appear overhead.

"Your dad's great," he said after a moment of comfortable silence. "He really loves you."

"I know. I'm lucky." She pulled her jacket tighter. "I didn't realize you two had gotten close."

"He's been...supportive. Good to talk to." He paused. "He cares a lot about your happiness and your future."

"He worries too much."

"He worries the right amount." He looked at her. "He mentioned you had a job interview with the county office."

"Oh. Yeah, it was Friday." She'd almost forgotten about it, her mind so focused on Charles. "It went well, actually. They seemed really interested."

"That's great." But something flickered across Charles' face that she couldn't make out. "That's really great, Aleece. You deserve good opportunities."

"It would mean staying in Timber Ridge," she said carefully, watching his reaction. "The job's here."

Charles' expression softened, and for a moment, she saw naked relief in his eyes. "Is that what you want? To stay?"

"I don't know. Maybe." She turned to face him more fully. "I used to think I needed to leave to prove I could make it somewhere else,

100

but lately I've been wondering if that was just running away from feeling like I didn't fit here."

"Do you feel like you fit now?"

The question hung between them. She thought about the past few weeks. Working on Charles' house, learning new skills, feeling useful and engaged, and present in a way she never had in college.

"More than I used to," she admitted. "Working on your house, building things...I feel like I'm actually doing something that matters. Creating something real."

"You are." Charles' voice was rough. "Every day you're there, you make that house more of what it's supposed to be."

"What is it supposed to be?"

"A home." He was looking at her with such intensity that it made her breath catch. "A real home."

"For whoever needs it?" She quoted that familiar phrase, frustrated. "Charles, you keep saying that. But who do you mean? Who are you building this for?"

"I want to tell you. I'm trying to—"

"Then just tell me!" Frustration boiled within her. "I don't understand why this is so hard. Why can't you just say what you're thinking, what you're feeling? We've been dancing around this for weeks, and I'm tired of not knowing what's happening between us."

"I know it's not fair to you." He turned to face her fully, and in the porch light, she could see conflict warring in his expression. "But I need you to understand everything before we move forward. I need you to know what you'd be choosing."

"Then help me understand. Explain it to me."

"Tomorrow," Charles said. "I promise. Tomorrow we'll talk, and I'll explain everything. About me, about shifters, about why this is complicated." He reached out, almost touching her hand, then pulled back. "I hope you choose what makes you happy, Aleece. Even if..."

"Even if what?" She caught his hand before he could withdraw it completely, holding it between both of hers. "Even if it's not you? Is that what you're trying to say?"

"Even if I can't offer you everything you deserve." His voice was barely above a whisper. "If what I am, what I can give you isn't enough."

"How can you think you're not enough?" She squeezed his hand. "Charles, you've been nothing but patient, kind, and generous with me. You've taught me so much, trusted me with something that clearly means everything to you. How could that not be enough?"

He looked at their joined hands, and when he spoke, his voice was thick with emotion. "Because there are things about being with a shifter and about being with *me* specifically that will change your life. Your future. I need you to understand what that means before you decide."

"What things? What are you talking about?"

But before he could answer, headlights swept across the porch. Her father's car pulled into the driveway, and Charles gently extracted his hand from hers.

"Tomorrow," he said again, standing. "I'll explain everything tomorrow. I promise."

She wanted to tell him, that's what he said the day before, but before she could, her father was out of the car and heading toward them.

Her father came up the porch steps, papers in hand. "Got them! Sorry that took so long. Did I miss anything?"

"No," she said, trying to keep the frustration from her voice. "Nothing."

"Well..." Charles stood. "It's been a long day, I should be going. Thomas, thank you for dinner. It was truly delicious."

"You're always welcome here." Her father nodded.

Charles nodded and headed toward his truck. At the bottom of the porch steps, he turned back, looking at her.

"Six o'clock tomorrow?" he asked. "For dinner at my place?"

"I'll be there."

"Okay." He smiled slightly. "To make up for all the waiting, I'll make something good."

She watched him drive away, then turned to her father. "Did you really need those papers?"

Her father had the grace to look sheepish. "I thought you two might want some time alone to talk."

"We were about to really talk, and then you came back."

"Ah." He winced. "Sorry. Bad timing?"

"The worst." She couldn't stay angry. "He wants to tell me something tomorrow. Something about being a shifter, about why this is complicated." She gestured vaguely.

His expression grew serious. "And you'll listen? Really listen, with an open mind?"

"Of course. Why wouldn't I?"

"Because what he tells you might change how you see things and how you see him." He put his hand on her shoulder. "Just promise me you'll hear him out completely before you make any decisions."

"You know what he's going to say, don't you?"

"I have suspicions, but it's not my place to explain. Charles needs to be the one to tell you." He squeezed her shoulder. "Just remember, whatever he tells you, it comes from a place of caring. He's trying to do right by you."

"I'm heading to my office to work on these papers." He held up whatever he had fetched before strolling into the house.

She sat there on the porch swing, her thoughts spinning.

I need you to know what you'd be choosing.

Whatever it was, whatever he needed to tell her, she'd listen, and then she'd decide. But as she sat in the darkness, she already knew what her decision would be.

She'd been choosing Charles for weeks now. Every time she picked up a tool to help him build, and every time she caught herself watching him work with that warm feeling in her chest.

She just needed to understand exactly what she was choosing and whether Charles would let himself be chosen.

CHAPTER 10
THE JOB OFFER

Monday morning, Aleece woke to two emails that could change everything.

The first was from the county office: *We're pleased to offer you the position of Administrative Coordinator...*

She sat up in bed, reading it twice to make sure she wasn't misunderstanding. They were offering her the job. Good salary, benefits, starting in three weeks. Everything she'd hoped for when she'd applied. It was a job in Timber Ridge, giving her a reason to stay.

I need to tell Charles.

She grabbed her phone, fingers hovering over his contact, then stopped. It was only seven in the morning. They also had dinner plans. She could tell him then, in person, and see his face when she shared the news.

Instead, she opened the second email, expecting another rejection from one of the city positions she'd applied to months ago.

Instead: *Congratulations! We are delighted to offer you a position with Sterling and Associates.*

She frowned, reading through the details. Sterling and Associates was a major consulting firm based in Denver. The position was Junior Business Analyst, with a starting salary that made her eyes widen. Significantly more than the county job. Plus benefits, plus a signing bonus, and opportunities for advancement. It was an incredible offer. There was just one problem: she didn't remember applying to Sterling and Associates.

She scrolled through her sent emails, searching. She'd applied to dozens of companies back in December, right after graduation, but she couldn't find Sterling and Associates anywhere in her records. Maybe she'd applied through a job board that had forwarded her resume?

She read the offer letter more carefully. Everything looked legitimate: official letterhead, a detailed job description, and the human resources agent's contact information. They wanted an answer within a week.

She set her phone down and stared at the ceiling. Two job offers. Both arrived on the same morning. One that would keep her in Timber Ridge, close to her father and the life she'd always known, and close to Charles.

The other would take her to Denver, into a career with real growth potential, the kind of opportunity most new graduates would kill for.

She should have been thrilled. Instead, she felt paralyzed. It was like she was looking at a crossroads, uncertain which to choose. Both brought their own types of risks and rewards. The question was what she truly wanted.

B y noon, Aleece still hadn't told anyone about either offer. She'd reread both emails a dozen times, made a pro-versus-con list that went nowhere, and worked herself into a state of anxious indecision. Finally, she texted Charles.

Can I come by earlier? Need to talk.

Of course. I'm here now.

She grabbed her coat and was in her car before she could overthink it, driving the familiar route to Charles' house on autopilot. Her thoughts spun with questions, with possibilities, with fears.

What if she chose wrong? If she stayed in Timber Ridge, would she spend the rest of her life wondering what she'd given up? What if she took the Denver job and spent the rest of her life homesick and miserable? Underneath it all, she wondered what Charles would want her to do.

His truck was in the driveway when she arrived, and he was on the porch before she'd even turned off her engine. The sight of him, solid, real, and concerned, made her chest loosen slightly.

"What's wrong?" he asked as she got out. "You sounded upset."

"I'm not upset. I'm just..." She climbed the porch steps. "I need to talk through something, and I thought you might help me see clearly."

"Okay." He gestured toward the door. "Come inside. I'll make coffee."

She followed him through the house, and as she did, she thought about all they'd done together. The idea of leaving this...leaving him settled into her stomach like a ball of lead. She joined him in the still unfinished but now functional kitchen, with the cabinets they'd installed. He made coffee while she perched on one of the sawhorses, organizing her thoughts.

"I got a job offer this morning," she finally said. "From the county for the position I interviewed for."

His whole body stilled, his back to her as he poured coffee. "That's great. Really great, Aleece."

"Yeah, it is. Good salary, benefits, and interesting work. I'd be coordinating community outreach programs, working with different departments." She accepted the mug he handed her. "I'd be staying in Timber Ridge."

"Is staying what you want?" His voice was carefully neutral as he leaned against the counter across from her.

"I think so. I mean, I've been leaning that way. Especially after these past few weeks, working here, feeling like I'm actually part of something." She took a sip of coffee. "But then I got another offer. Same day. Sterling and Associates in Denver."

Pain flickered across Charles' face. "Denver."

"It's a really good offer, Charles. Better salary, a fancy title, and better advancement opportunities. The kind of position that could really launch a career." She set down her mug. "The thing is, I don't remember applying to them. Which is weird, right?"

"Maybe you applied through a job board? Sometimes companies find candidates that way."

"Maybe." But something about it still bothered her. "I just...I suddenly have two very different paths in front of me, and I don't know which one to choose."

He was quiet for a long moment, staring into his coffee. "What does your gut tell you?"

"That's the problem. My gut is giving me conflicting signals." She rubbed her temples. "Part of me thinks I should take the Denver job. It's objectively the better opportunity. More money and prestige, along with a better resume builder. Isn't that what you're supposed to do after college? Take the best opportunity available?"

"Is that what you think you're supposed to do? Or what you actually want to do?"

"I don't know anymore." Her voice came out frustrated. "A few months ago, the answer would have been clear. Take the better job, build the best career, and prove I can make it in the bigger world. But now..."

"Now?" he prompted gently.

"Now I'm not sure that's what success looks like for me." She met his gaze. "These past few weeks, working on your house, I've been happier than I was all four years of college. Is that crazy? To be happier doing manual labor in an unfinished house than I was pursuing my degree?"

"It's not crazy. It means you were doing something that actually engaged you. That mattered to you." His expression was unreadable. "But that doesn't mean you should give up career opportunities. At the county job, you could do meaningful work, too. Community outreach, helping people. That's not settling, that's making a difference in the community."

"I know, and I want to take it. I think." She slid off the sawhorse, too restless to sit still. "But what if I'm only choosing it because I want to stay here? What if I'm deciding based on not wanting to leave instead of actually wanting the job?"

"Would that be so wrong?"

"I don't know. Maybe? I just..." She turned to face him. "Charles, I need to know. Is there a reason I should stay? Besides the job?"

The question hung in the air between them. He stared at her, and she saw him struggling with something internal. "Aleece—"

"Because if there is, if you...if we..." She took a step toward him. "I need to know that I'm not imagining this thing between us. That it's real and worth considering when I'm making this decision."

He set down his coffee mug carefully, like he didn't trust his hands. "You're not imagining it."

"Then tell me. Help me understand what we are, what we could be, because I can't make this decision without all the facts. I need to know—"

"You can't make this decision based on me." His voice was rough. "Your career and future are too important to base on whatever this is between us."

The words hit like a slap. "Whatever this is? Is that really how you see it?"

"That's not what I meant." He ran a hand through his hair, frustrated. "I just mean we haven't even talked yet about everything and what being with me would mean. You can't factor that into a career decision when you don't even know—"

"Then tell me now! We were supposed to talk tonight anyway. Just tell me whatever it is you've been holding back, and then I can make an informed decision."

"It's not that simple."

"Why not?" Her voice rose. "Why does everything with you have to be so complicated? Why can't you just be honest about what you want?"

"Because what I want doesn't matter." His voice matched hers, frustration breaking through his usual control. "What matters is what's right for you. Your future and your life are too important for me to influence with my feelings."

"Your feelings," she repeated. "So, you do have feelings. About me. About us."

He closed his eyes. "Of course I do."

"Then say it. Say what you want. Let me factor that into my decision."

"I want..." He opened his eyes, and the raw emotion there took her breath away. "I want you to choose what makes you happy and what gives you the life you deserve, even if that takes you away from here. From me."

Tears pricked her eyes. "That's not an answer. That's you being noble and self-sacrificing and completely infuriating."

"I'm trying to do what's right."

"By pushing me away? By refusing to tell me how you feel?" She stepped closer to stand right in front of him now. "Charles, I'm falling for you. I think I have been since that first day you came to fix the pipes. I think, no, I know, you feel the same way. So why won't you admit it?"

He reached up, almost touching her arms, but he caught himself. "Because once I do, once we start this, there's no going back. I need you to know what you're getting into first. I need you to understand—"

"Then tell me! Right now. Whatever it is you think I need to know, just say it."

"I can't." Anguish laced his voice. "Not like this. Not when you're trying to make a huge career decision, and everything is confused and complicated. I won't be responsible for you choosing wrong because I influenced you at the wrong moment."

"So what, I'm supposed to make this decision without knowing where we stand? Without understanding what I might be staying for or leaving behind?"

"Yes." His voice was firm despite the pain in his eyes. "Because your career has to be about you. Not about a man you've known for less than two months, or about a relationship that doesn't even fully exist yet."

The words were logical and rational. Everything she had been taught about making important decisions. They also felt completely wrong.

"I can't believe you're doing this," she said quietly. "I finally ask you directly, finally put myself out there, and you're still holding back."

"I'm trying to protect you."

"I don't need protecting! I need honesty!" Her voice broke. "I need you to tell me the truth about what you want so I can make an actual informed decision instead of guessing, hoping, and wondering."

"I can't make this decision for you, Aleece. I won't."

"I'm not asking you to make it for me. I'm asking you to be part of the equation. To let me consider all the factors instead of pretending the biggest one doesn't exist."

They stared at each other, both breathing hard, the space between them charged with frustration and hurt and longing.

"These job offers, they change things. The timeline I had planned, the conversation we were supposed to have tonight—" He shook his head. "You need clarity for this decision, and I can't give you half-truths or partial information. It wouldn't be fair."

"So, what are you saying?"

"I'm saying, make your decision based on what you know. The jobs, the locations, and what each opportunity offers for your career." His voice was steady now, carefully controlled. "Don't factor me in. Don't let whatever is or isn't between us influence something this important."

"And after? After I decide?"

"After you decide, we'll talk. I'll tell you everything. And then..." He trailed off.

"Then what?"

"Then you'll know whether staying or coming back is something you actually want."

Tears spilled over and trailed down her cheeks. "You're really going to make me do this alone? Make this decision without knowing—"

"I'm making you do it for yourself," he interrupted gently. "Not for me, or us, or any possibility of a future. For you and your career."

"What if I don't want to do it alone?"

"You're not alone. You have your father, your friends, and most of all your own judgment. But you can't have me weighing in. Not on this. It wouldn't be right."

She wiped her eyes angrily. "I hate that you're being logical about this."

"I know."

"I hate that you're probably right."

"I know that too."

She looked at him and saw the conflict in his eyes, the tension in his shoulders, and the way his hands were clenched at his sides like he was physically restraining himself from reaching for her. He was sacrificing what he wanted for what he thought was best for her. Being noble, selfless, and downright infuriating. She couldn't hate him for it, even though she wanted to.

"I should go," she said quietly. "I guess I should think about this. Both offers."

"Yeah." He didn't move. "For what it's worth, either choice would be a good one. County job or Denver. You'd succeed at both."

"That doesn't help."

"I know."

She grabbed her bag from where she had dropped it and headed for the door. At the threshold, she turned back. He was standing in the kitchen, looking lost and miserable in the house he'd been building with such hope.

"Charles?"

"Yeah?"

"When we do talk, when I've made my decision, and you tell me everything, don't hold back. Don't protect me or try to make it easier, just tell me the truth. All of it. I deserve that much."

"You deserve everything." He nodded. "I promise. When we talk, you'll get the whole truth. No matter what."

She left before she could change her mind and demanded answers she knew he wouldn't give.

Aleece barely made it through the door before her father questioned her.

"What happened? You're back already. What happened to dinner with Charles?" He stood in the doorway to his office.

"I got two job offers. One here, one in Denver, and Charles refuses to tell me how he feels because he doesn't want to influence my decision." She shook her head and collapsed onto the sofa. "He's being noble and logical, and I want to strangle him."

Her father sat beside her. "He's doing what he thinks is right."

"I know. That's what makes it so infuriating." She wiped her eyes. "Dad, what do I do? How do I make this decision when the biggest factor is something I'm specifically not supposed to consider?"

"You consider everything else. The jobs themselves, the locations, what each path offers. You trust that whatever you choose, the right things will fall into place."

"What if they don't?"

"Then you adjust and make a different choice. Life isn't just one decision, sweetheart. It's a series of them." He squeezed her shoulder. "But for what it's worth, I think you already know what you want. You're just scared to admit it."

She thought about that. The county job in Timber Ridge, coming home every evening to this house and potentially to Charles. Then there was the Denver job, starting over in a city where she'd struggled before, and chasing opportunities that looked good on paper but might feel hollow in reality.

"I do know," she admitted quietly. "I'm just not sure if I'm choosing it for the right reasons."

"There are no wrong reasons. Just your reasons." Her father stood. "Sleep on it. Both offers give you time to decide. Don't rush just because you feel pressured."

While her father wandered off to his office, she lay there on the sofa, thinking about both offer letters. She'd read them so many times she had them memorized.

The county job would allow her to do meaningful work, have a community impact, and stay in Timber Ridge. She'd be near her father, the life she'd always known, and Charles.

Denver offered career advancement, a higher salary, and the chance to prove she could make it in the bigger world, away from Timber Ridge and everything familiar. It also meant she'd be away from Charles and whatever was developing between them.

When she put it like that, the choice seemed obvious.

But Charles' words echoed in her mind: *Don't factor me in. Don't let whatever is or isn't between us influence something this important.*

Could she do that? Could she really make this decision without considering him?

CHAPTER 11

THE STRANGER ARRIVES

T hree days had passed since the job offers arrived, and Aleece still hadn't made a decision. She'd asked both employers for more time. The county had readily agreed, while Sterling and Associates had reluctantly given her until the end of the week.

She hadn't been back to Charles' house, and besides a few brief text messages, they hadn't spoken. The distance felt wrong, but she needed space to think clearly, and being around him made clarity impossible.

She sat at the kitchen table, staring at her laptop without seeing it, when her father came home early. The sound of the front door closing hard, not quite a slam but close, made her look up.

"Dad?"

He appeared in the kitchen doorway, and the expression on his face immediately put her on alert. He looked tense, jaw tight, with an edge to his movements that she rarely saw. Her father was usually calm, measured, the steady presence everyone in Timber Ridge relied on.

"What's wrong?" She closed her laptop.

"We need to talk." Her father moved to the sink, poured himself a glass of water, drank it, then turned to face her. "A shifter came to town today. Asking about you."

"What? Who?"

"Someone from out of state. He went to the town hall first to ask questions. Where you lived, who raised you, and how to find you." His hands clenched on the counter. "Sally called me immediately. She thought I should know someone was poking around."

"What did he want?" she asked.

"To talk to you. Said he has information about your family. Your biological family."

The world seemed to tilt slightly, and she gripped the edge of the table. "Did he say who he was?"

Her father's expression was grim. "He claims to be your father. Robert Way."

The name meant nothing to her. She'd spent twenty-two years not knowing her biological parents' names, and now one was suddenly here, real, asking for her.

"My biological father," she repeated numbly.

"That's what he says. I haven't confirmed it yet." He moved to sit across from her. "Aleece, I need you to listen to me. Something feels off about this. The timing, the way he showed up asking questions instead of reaching out directly—"

"Maybe he didn't know how to approach me."

"Maybe. Or maybe there's another reason he's here." He watched her for a moment. "I met with him briefly. Told him he couldn't just show up in town demanding information about *my* daughter without going through me first."

"What did he say?"

"That he understood. He's been searching for you and finally tracked you to Timber Ridge. Said he wants to make amends, be part of your life." Her father paused. "Said your mother would have wanted him to find you."

She felt tears prick her eyes at the mention of her mother, but blinked them away. "Did he say anything about her? About why they gave me up?"

"Not much. Just that she died a few years ago, and that he's been looking for you ever since. He wants to make it right by her."

"She's dead?" The words felt hollow. She had never known her mother, but some part of her had always held hope that maybe one day she'd find her, understand why she'd been left behind. "When?"

"He didn't say exactly. Aleece—" Her father reached across the table, covering her hand with his. "I know you have questions. You've wanted to know about your biological parents your whole life, but I'm asking you to be cautious here. Let me do some background checks first, so I can make sure this man is who he says he is."

"You don't trust him."

"I don't know him. And I don't like that he showed up out of nowhere right when you're making big life decisions." His grip tightened slightly. "It might be a coincidence, or it might not be."

"What else would it be?"

"I don't know. That's what worries me. Look, I'm not saying don't meet him. If he really is your father, you deserve to know your history. I'm just saying, be careful. Don't trust him immediately just because he's offering answers you've wanted."

She pulled her hand back and wrapped her arms around herself. "I need to meet him. I need to at least hear what he has to say."

"I know." He didn't look happy about it. "Just promise me you'll be smart. Meet him in public, don't go anywhere alone with him until we know more. If anything feels wrong, you leave. Immediately."

"Okay. I promise."

"And Aleece?" Her father's voice was softer now. "Whatever he tells you, whatever story he gives, remember that I'm your father. I raised you. That doesn't change."

Tears spilled over. "I know, Dad. This doesn't change anything between us."

"Good." He stood, pulling her into a hug. "I'll set up a meeting. Tomorrow at the diner. Public, safe. I'll be there too."

"Dad—"

"Non-negotiable. You want to meet him, I'm there. At least for the first time."

She nodded against his shoulder, too overwhelmed to argue. Her biological father was here in Timber Ridge, and he wanted to see her after twenty-two years.

"I'll set it up now." He stepped back from her, and she stood there, too shocked to move.

After he left to make the calls necessary, she sat down at the table and tried to process everything that was happening. Her thoughts were spinning with questions: What did Robert Way look like? Did she have his eyes, his features? What had her mother been like? Why had they given her up? Where had they been all these years? Underneath it all: Why now? Why show up now, when her life was already in upheaval, when she was trying to make impossible decisions about her future?

Her phone sat on the table, and before she could think better of it, she called Charles.

He answered on the second ring. "Aleece? Is everything okay?"

Just hearing his voice eased some of the tension in her chest. "I need to tell you something."

"What happened?"

"My biological father...he's here, in Timber Ridge. He wants to meet me."

There was silence on the other end for a long moment. "When?"

"Thomas is setting it up. At the diner tomorrow, I'm guessing." She stood, pacing to the window. "I don't know what to think. I've wondered about him my whole life. Now he's suddenly here, and I don't know how to feel."

"That's understandable. This is huge." His voice was gentle. "How are you holding up?"

"I'm scared, angry, and curious. All at once." She pressed her forehead against the cool glass. "What if he tells me something I don't want to know? What if the reason they gave me up was..." She couldn't finish the sentence.

"Whatever the reason was, it wasn't because of you. We've talked about this."

"I know. But what if I'm wrong? What if there really was something about me that made them not want me?"

"Aleece." His voice was firm. "Stop. There's nothing about you that would make anyone not want you. Nothing. Whatever happened, whatever decisions your parents made, that was about their circumstances, not your worth."

She wanted to believe him. "Charles, I'm terrified."

"I know. Do you want me there? When you meet him?"

Gratitude and longing filled her. "You'd do that?"

"Of course. If you need support, I'm there."

Aleece closed her eyes, tempted. Having Charles there would make everything easier. "I think I need to do this alone first. Well, with my dad...Thomas, I mean. But family only, you know?"

The pause that followed was weighted. "I understand."

"It's not that I don't want you there—"

"Aleece, it's fine. Really. This is a family thing. I get it." But there was something in his voice that made her think he was hurt, even if he was trying to hide it.

"Charles—"

"Call me after? Let me know how it goes?"

"Of course."

"And Aleece? Your dad's right to be cautious. I don't want to make you paranoid, but...be careful, okay? If anything feels off, trust your instincts."

"You don't trust him either."

"I don't know him. And the timing..." He trailed off. "Just be careful. That's all I'm saying."

After they hung up, she stood at the window, watching clouds gather over the mountains. Everyone was warning her to be careful and not to trust too quickly. But this was her biological father. He had supposedly been searching for her and wanted to make amends. Didn't she owe it to herself to at least hear him out?

Thursday morning dawned gray and cold. Aleece changed outfits four times before settling on jeans and a sweater, casual but put together. She wanted to look like she had her life together, even though she felt like she was falling apart.

Her father drove them to the diner in silence. She appreciated that he didn't try to fill the space with empty reassurances or warnings. He'd said what he needed to. Now he was just there, solid and supportive, the father who'd actually raised her.

The diner was moderately busy for mid-morning. Mrs. Appleton greeted them at the door, her expression sympathetic. Her father had clearly filled her in.

"He's in the back booth," she said quietly, gesturing toward the corner.

Aleece's heart hammered as she turned to look.

Robert Way sat in the booth, a cup of coffee in front of him, watching them approach. Even with him sitting, she could tell he was tall, with dark hair graying at the temples. His features were sharp, patrician, with an air of confidence that bordered on arrogance. He was well-dressed, with an expensive watch, everything about him screaming money and status.

He stood as they approached, and she saw her father tense beside her.

"Aleece," Robert said, and his voice was smooth, cultured. "Thank you for agreeing to meet. I know this must be overwhelming."

She slid into the booth across from him, and her father sat protectively beside her. Up close, she searched Robert's face for any trace of herself. The eyes were wrong—his were gray where hers were brown. The nose was different. But there was something in the shape of the face, the line of the jaw, that might have been familiar. Or might have been wishful thinking.

"You said you're my biological father," she said, proud of how steady her voice was.

"I am." Robert pulled out his wallet and extracted a folded piece of paper. He passed it across the table. "This is your original birth certificate. Before it was sealed by the state."

She unfolded it with shaking hands. There, in faded ink: *Aleece Marie Way. Mother: Mary Bran. Father: Robert Way.*

Her name. Her real, original name.

"Mary," Aleece whispered. "My mother's name was Mary."

"Yes." Robert's expression softened slightly. "She was beautiful and kind. You have her eyes."

She looked up sharply. "But—"

"Your eyes are brown like hers. But your eyes, your smile, that's all, Mary."

Beside her, Dad was rigid, watching every move Robert made. She could feel his protective energy radiating outward.

"Why?" The question came out before she could stop it. "Why did you give me up? Why leave me in Timber Ridge in January, where I could have died?" Her voice broke.

Robert's expression turned pained. "We didn't have a choice. Well, I didn't. Mary—" He stopped, seemed to struggle with something. "The situation was complicated. We were young, unprepared. My family, my clan, they didn't approve of Mary. She was human, and I was expected to mate within my own kind."

"So, you chose your pack over your child." Dad's voice was cold.

"I chose wrong," Robert said sharply. "I know that now. I made decisions then that I've regretted every day since. But I thought..." He looked at Aleece. "Mary thought you'd be better off here, in Timber Ridge, where shifters and humans coexist peacefully. That way, if you were a shifter, you'd be around your own kind. If you weren't, I knew they'd take care of you as one of their own. Here I knew you'd be found and cared for, and you were. Thomas gave you a good life."

"A life you weren't part of," she said.

"No, and I'm sorry for that. More sorry than you can know." Robert leaned forward. "But I'm here now. I want to make amends. I want to know my daughter."

"Twenty-two years later." She couldn't keep the bitterness out of her voice. "Why now? Why not five years ago, or ten, or fifteen?"

Robert's eyes darkened, and his back straightened. "I've been looking for you for over a year. It took time to find you. The records were sealed, and you were unofficially placed with Thomas. I didn't know Mary had brought you to Timber Ridge until I found a newspaper clipping from here. Even then, it took resources and persistence."

"You said Mary died. When?"

"Three years ago." Robert's voice was flat. "Heart failure. She was only forty-five."

She did the math. Her mother had been twenty-three when she was born. Had spent twenty-two years without her daughter, then died young. The information sat like lead in her stomach.

"Did she ever try to find me?"

Robert was quiet for a long moment. "She thought about you every day, but she believed you were better off without us. Without the complications of shifter politics and pack rivalries."

"That's not an answer," Thomas interjected. "Did she try to find her daughter or not?"

"No," Robert admitted. "She didn't. She thought it would be selfish. That bringing you into our world would only hurt you. She died believing you were surrounded by a family that loved you and didn't need the complication of having us in your life after all that time."

The first tear slipped down her cheek. Her mother had thought about her but never tried to find her and had died believing Aleece was better off without her.

"I don't understand," she whispered. "If she cared, if you both cared, how could you just leave me? How could you go twenty-two years without—"

"Because we were cowards," Robert said bluntly. "We made the easy choice instead of the right one. By the time I realized that, by the time I decided to find you, Mary was gone, and you were grown. But I'm here now. I want to be part of your life, if you'll let me. I want to make up for lost time."

She wiped her eyes, trying to process everything. This man was her father, but he was also a stranger. He had answers to questions she'd been asking her whole life, but the answers weren't what she'd hoped for. There was no dramatic reason, no unavoidable circumstance that had forced them to give her up. Just fear. Just choosing the easy path over the hard one.

"I need time," she said finally. "To think about all this."

"Of course." Robert pulled out a business card. "I'm staying at the inn for a few days. Call me when you're ready to talk more. I have stories about your mother, photos, and things that belonged to her that I brought for you."

She took the card with numb fingers. Robert Way, CEO, Way Enterprises. A Denver address.

Denver.

"You live in Denver?" she asked.

"Yes. Have for years. It's where my company is based."

"What kind of company?"

"Real estate development. Commercial properties mostly." Robert smiled slightly. "I've done quite well for myself. Which means I can offer you opportunities, Aleece. Help you get started in whatever career you choose. I have connections throughout Colorado—"

"That's enough," Thomas said, standing abruptly. "Aleece has opportunities. She doesn't need your connections or your money."

Robert held up his hands. "I'm not trying to buy my way into her life. I'm just offering to help. What father wouldn't want to help his daughter?"

"The father who raised her," Thomas said coldly. "That's who. Come on, Aleece. We're done here."

She stood on shaky legs, clutching the business card and birth certificate. Robert stood as well.

"I hope you'll call," he said. "I really do want to know you. To be the father I should have been all along."

She nodded but couldn't form words. Her father put his arm around her and guided her out of the diner. His hand was solid and warm on her shoulder, grounding her.

In the truck, she stared at the birth certificate until the words blurred. Aleece Marie Way. A name she'd never known, just like the parents she'd never had.

"You okay?" Her father asked gently.

"I don't know." Aleece folded the certificate carefully. "He lives in Denver, Dad. Denver."

"I caught that."

"He wants to help with my career. Has connections." She looked at him. "That's too convenient, isn't it? That he shows up right when I'm deciding between staying here and going to Denver?"

"It struck me as suspicious, yes."

"Do you think..." She hesitated. "Do you think he had something to do with that job offer? Sterling and Associates?"

His jaw clenched. "I don't know. But I'm going to find out."

They drove home in silence, and when they arrived, she went straight to her room. She grabbed her computer and pulled up the Sterling and Associates offer letter, reading it more carefully now. The salary was unusually high for an entry-level position, the benefits were exceptional, and now that she thought about it, the whole thing had felt too good to be true.

Her phone rang, and she glanced down at the screen to see Charles' name on the display.

"Hi."

"How did it go?" he asked as soon as she answered.

"I don't know. It was..." She sank onto her bed. "Charles, he lives in Denver, and I think he might have something to do with that job offer."

Charles mumbled something under his breath that she couldn't make out. "Tell me everything."

"He claims he's been looking for me for a year. That he and my biological mother, Mary, gave me up because it wasn't fair to bring me into the complications of shifter politics and pack rivalries. He claimed he didn't have a choice, and that's why they gave me up. The situation was complicated. We were young, unprepared. Family and clan, they didn't approve of Mary because she was human, and they didn't want me around them." She took a breath before adding. "But he tried to use his connections to bribe me."

As she rambled, Charles listened without interrupting, and when she finished, he was quiet for a long moment.

"Aleece, I need to tell you something," he finally said.

"What?"

"About shifter culture and why Thomas and I have both been suspicious." His voice was careful. "There are political reasons a shifter might want to reconnect with a grown child. Especially a child who's been raised in Timber Ridge. It gives them..."

"Access," she finished, understanding clicking into place. "Dad said something about that. About me being from Timber Ridge, giving him an in somehow."

"Yeah. Your dad's position as mayor, the respect the community has for him...I'm saying if Robert could claim kinship, use you as a connection—"

"He could do business here that he might not be able to otherwise." She finished for him.

"Exactly." He paused. "I'm not saying that's definitely what's happening. Maybe he's genuine, and he really does want to make amends. But the timing, the Denver job offer, the way he's offering to help your career..."

"It's manipulation," she said flatly. "He's trying to get me to Denver, where he can control me, and use me as leverage somehow."

"I don't know that for sure. But I want you to be careful. Don't make any decisions based on what he's offering until you know what he really wants."

After they hung up, she sat on her bed, staring at Robert Way's business card. Her biological father, the man she'd wondered about her whole life, was possibly using her and trying to manipulate her into making decisions that would benefit him.

The county job offer, the one she'd been leaning toward, suddenly felt even more right. But first, she needed to confirm something.

She grabbed her laptop from the nightstand, pulled up the Sterling and Associates website, and searched for information about the company. It took some digging, but she finally found it: Way Enterprises was listed as a major investor in Sterling and Associates' parent company. Robert Way had arranged the job offer and had used his connections to dangle an opportunity in front of her, trying to lure her to Denver.

The realization made her feel sick. Her biological father didn't want to know her. He wanted to use her, and she'd almost fallen for it.

CHAPTER 12
DIGGING INTO THE PAST

A leece spent Friday night unable to sleep, the birth certificate and business card spread on her nightstand like evidence of a crime. Questions cycled through her thoughts on endless repeat. Had Robert really loved her mother? Why had Mary never tried to find her? What did Robert actually want from her? All of it made her wonder how much of her life had been shaped by decisions other people made without her knowledge.

Around midnight, she gave up on sleep and tiptoed downstairs. Her father was in his study, reading. He'd always been a night owl.

"Can't sleep either?" he asked, looking up.

She curled into the chair across from his desk. "Tell me about when you found me. Everything you remember."

He set down his book, his expression soft with old memories. "It was January fifteenth. Bitter cold that night, well below zero. I got a call around two in the morning from the fire station. They'd found a baby on their steps, bundled in blankets, with a note."

"Can I see it? The note?" She knew her father would have saved it.

He pulled open a drawer and extracted a worn manila folder.

Inside was a plastic sleeve protecting a piece of paper. The ink faded, but it was still legible.

Please take care of her. I can't. She deserves better than what I can give her. Safety. Her name is Aleece. She was born on January third. I'm so sorry.

Aleece traced the words through the plastic, trying to imagine her mother writing them. The handwriting was shaky, rushed. Desperate.

"That's all?" she whispered. "No explanation why?"

"That's all." Thomas' voice was gentle. "The authorities searched for your parents, of course. But with no last name, no real leads, they couldn't find anything. After six months of trying, they closed the case. You became mine officially."

"Did anyone ever come looking? Years later?"

"No." He shook his head. "I always thought they might. Hoped they would, honestly, so you could have answers, but no one ever came."

Until now. Until Robert Way showed up twenty-two years later with convenient timing and carefully crafted stories.

"Dad, what do you know about shifter pack politics? About human-shifter relationships?"

His expression grew guarded, and his back straightened. "Why?"

"Robert said his clan didn't approve of Mary. That they didn't accept human-shifter pairings. Is that true? Is that a thing?"

"It can be in some packs. More traditional ones, especially." Dad leaned forward. "But Aleece, most modern packs have evolved beyond that. Plenty of shifters have human partners. It's not the scandal it might have been thirty years ago."

"But it could have been the reason? For giving me up?"

"Maybe. Or maybe that's just the story Robert wants you to believe." He held her gaze. "I don't trust him, sweetheart. Everything about this feels calculated."

"I know. But he's my biological father. He has answers I've wanted my whole life. Shouldn't I at least hear him out?"

"You already did. You met him, heard his story."

"He said he has more. Photos of my mother, stories about her, things that belonged to her." Her voice cracked. "Don't I deserve to know about her? Even if Robert's motives aren't pure?"

Her father sat there quietly for a long moment. "You do deserve answers. Just promise me you'll be careful. Meet him in public, don't let him isolate you, and trust your instincts. If anything feels wrong—"

"I'll leave. I promise."

Like her father, she didn't trust Robert, but she also wanted more answers than he'd given during their short meeting at the café.

The next morning, Aleece texted Robert.

Can we meet? I have questions about my mother.

His response came within minutes.

Of course. Lunch today? There's a nice place in Meadow Haven, the next town over. More private than Timber Ridge.

More private. Away from her father's watchful eye and the protective community that had raised her. Every instinct told her it was a bad idea.

Okay. Noon.

She agreed anyway, but at least she picked the lunch hour rush, ensuring plenty of people around.

Nervously, she tried to keep herself busy, but eventually she gave up and headed downstairs to tell her father. He was already sitting at the table with coffee, likely his third cup by now, reading over some papers. "Morning."

"Morning, sweetheart. There's coffee in the pot."

She poured a cup of coffee and sat down at the table with her father. "Dad..."

"Yes?" He set the papers aside, his attention solely focused on her. "I know it's serious when you want to talk before you've had coffee."

"I'm..." She stumbled over her words as she stared down into the mug of dark liquid, searching for answers. "I'm meeting Robert in Meadow Haven at noon."

"You're really going to meet him alone? In another town?" It was clear from his tone that he didn't like the idea.

"I need to know about Mary. If I bring you, he'll just clam up. Say what he thinks you want to hear instead of the truth."

"The *truth* he tells you might not be the real truth either."

"I know. But it's the only truth I'm going to get." Forgetting the coffee, she stood and kissed his cheek. "I'll text you when I get there and when I'm leaving. If you don't hear from me, send the cavalry."

"That's not funny."

"Little bit funny."

But he didn't smile, she saw only concern in his dark honey-brown eyes.

Not knowing what else to say, she headed for the entryway, grabbed her coat and keys before glancing back at him. "I love you, Dad."

"I love you, too, Aleece. Drive safely and be careful."

With one last long look at him, she headed out the door to her car. As she started the engine, her heart seemed to skip a beat. *Am I doing the right thing? This is crazy, isn't it?* Despite the doubt, she backed out of the driveway and headed out of town.

The drive to Meadow Haven took twenty minutes. The restaurant Robert had chosen was upscale—white tablecloths, leather booths, the kind of place where entrees cost more than she usually spent on groceries for a week when she was living in Denver.

Robert was already there, standing when she approached. He'd dressed for the occasion—suit jacket, pressed shirt, looking every inch the successful businessman.

"Aleece. Thank you for coming." He gestured to the booth. "Please sit. Order anything you like."

The waiter appeared immediately, clearly primed by Robert.

"Water and a chicken Ceaser salad." She didn't trust her nervous stomach with anything heavier.

"Filet, rare, and the house wine, red." Robert leaned back against the booth. Comfortable and confident in this expensive setting.

This is his world. Money, power, and control.

"I brought these for you," Robert said once the waiter left, pulling a manila envelope from his briefcase. "Photos of your mother. Some from before you were born, some from after. I thought you'd want to see them."

She took the envelope and, with shaking hands, opened it. The first photo made her gasp.

Mary, her biological mother, was beautiful. Dark hair, warm brown eyes, a smile that looked like it came easily. She was young in the photo, maybe twenty, standing in a park somewhere with sunlight in her hair.

"That was taken a year before you were born," Robert said quietly. "In Denver. She loved that park."

The next photo showed Mary holding a baby. Not any baby, she was holding Aleece. Mary looked tired but radiant, gazing down at the infant in her arms with such love that it made Aleece's throat tight.

"The day after you were born," Robert said. "At the hospital."

"She looks happy." She traced the image, trying to reconcile this loving mother with the one who'd left her on the fire station steps less than two weeks later.

"She was. You were perfect. Healthy and beautiful. Mary was over the moon." Robert's voice held an edge of something that might have been genuine regret. "But reality set in quickly. My family wasn't pleased. Started making threats and demands. I had to choose."

"Between them and us."

"Yes." He took a sip of wine. "I was young, Aleece. Twenty-five. Still dependent on my family's clan and their resources. I didn't have the strength then to stand up to them. To fight for you and Mary the way I should have."

The food arrived, giving Aleece time to absorb this. She pushed her salad around her plate, appetite gone.

"So what happened? Why leave me in Timber Ridge specifically?"

"That was Mary's idea. I didn't know that's where she left you until after she passed." He cut into his steak with precise movements. "She'd heard about Timber Ridge. A town where shifters and humans coexisted peacefully, where the mayor himself had a reputation for kindness. She thought you'd be safe there. Protected."

"Protected from what?"

He was quiet for a moment. "From my clan. From the complications of being born to a shifter father and a human mother. You have to understand that pack politics and rivalries could have put you in danger."

The story sounded reasonable. Logical even. But something about the way Robert told it made her instincts prickle. It was too smooth, too rehearsed.

"You said Mary died three years ago. How?"

"Heart failure, officially. But honestly?" He set down his fork. "I think she died of a broken heart. She never got over giving you up. Never forgave herself for leaving you."

The words hit like a punch, but the doubt lingered. "She spent twenty-two years regretting it, but never tried to find me?"

"She was afraid that bringing you into our world would only hurt you more. That you were better off with the life you had." He leaned forward. "But I don't have those fears anymore. My clan...I'm the alpha now. I have power, resources, and connections. I can offer you everything Mary wanted to but couldn't."

"Like the job in Denver?"

He smiled, but it didn't quite reach his eyes. "You figured that out."

"Your company is invested in Sterling and Associates. You arranged that offer." She set down her fork. "Why?"

"You're my daughter, and I want to help you succeed. I have connections throughout Colorado. I can open doors for you that would otherwise be closed." He pulled out his phone and showed her a luxury apartment building. "I own this property in downtown Denver. You could live there rent-free while you establish yourself. The Sterling and Associates position would be the beginning. With my guidance, you could go anywhere, do anything."

It was too convenient. Too perfectly designed to appeal to an ambitious new graduate looking for opportunities.

"What do you get out of this?" she asked bluntly.

He looked genuinely surprised. "I get to know my daughter and make up for lost time."

"And?" It felt like there was more, even if he wasn't saying it.

"And nothing." But there was something in his expression that told her there was definitely an "and."

"You want something from me. Something besides just 'getting to know me.' What is it?"

He sat back, reassessing her. "You're sharp. I like that. Mary was like that, too. She could see through bullshit from a mile away."

"Answer the question."

"Fine. Yes, there's a business angle." His tone shifted, becoming more businesslike. "I've been trying to develop property in Timber Ridge for years. It's a prime location. Growing population, tourism potential, everything I need, but the town council keeps blocking my proposals. Your father, Thomas, has been the main opposition."

Understanding clicked into place. "You want to use me to get to him. To influence the council."

"I want us to have a relationship that could benefit both of us. You get opportunities, connections, and a chance at a real career. I get—"

"Access to Timber Ridge." Aleece stood abruptly. "That's what this is about. Not making amends, not getting to know your daughter. You want to use me as leverage against Thomas."

"Sit down, Aleece. You're being dramatic."

"I'm being honest. Which is more than you've been." She grabbed the envelope of photos. "Thank you for these. For the information about Mary. But I'm not interested in being your pawn."

"You're making a mistake." Robert's voice hardened. "I'm offering you real opportunities. A chance at a life beyond that small town. Beyond the limitations of—"

"Of what? Being raised by someone who actually wanted me?" Tears prick her eyes, but she refused to let them fall. "Thomas has been more of a father to me than you'll ever be."

"Thomas is a good man, I'm sure, but he's limited you. Kept you in Timber Ridge, raised you with small-town values and dreams. I can offer you more."

"I don't want more from you." She started to leave, then turned back. "One more question. About Mary. Did she really want to leave me? Or did you make her?"

His expression went carefully blank. "What are you implying?"

"I'm asking if my mother had a choice. If leaving me was her decision or yours."

The silence stretched between them, heavy with unspoken truths.

"Mary did what she thought was best."

"That's not an answer."

"It's the only answer you're going to get."

"It's an answer all in itself. If you hadn't forced her to abandon me, you'd have said so." She shook her head. "It was your decision, and you won't admit it now because you're hoping I overlook it and allow you to use me."

With that, she turned and headed for the door, ignoring him as he called her name. She made it to her car before the tears came, angry, frustrated, and heartbroken all at once.

She'd wanted answers about her mother, and instead she'd gotten confirmation that Robert was using her. He'd arranged the Denver job offer as bait, and everything he'd said was calculated to manipulate her into doing what he wanted. But worse was the suspicion that Mary might not have wanted to leave her at all. That Robert had made that decision for them.

She pulled out her phone with shaking hands and called her father.

"I'm okay," she said as soon as he answered. "But you were right about everything. He arranged the Denver job offer. He wants to use me to get access to Timber Ridge."

"Are you safe? Where are you?"

"Still in Meadow Haven. In my car, but I'm leaving now. I'm coming *home*." As she said the last word, she realized that's exactly what Timber Ridge was. It was home.

"Come straight home. We need to talk."

The drive back to Timber Ridge passed in a blur. Her thought spun with revelations, half-truths, and the sinking realization that she'd probably never know the whole truth about why she'd been left. But one thing was clear: Robert Way wasn't interested in being her father. He was interested in what she could do for him.

When she pulled into the driveway, her father was waiting. He was at her car door before she could get out. As she stood, he wrapped her in a hug.

"I'm sorry, sweetheart. I'm sorry he turned out to be exactly what I was afraid he was."

"He said something," she mumbled against his shoulder. "About Mary and about whether leaving me was really her choice."

He pulled back, his expression grim. "What did he say?"

"He wouldn't answer directly. Just said she did what she thought was best." She wiped her eyes. "But the way he said it...Dad, I don't think she wanted to leave me. I think he made her. I told him as much when I left, too."

"We'll never know for sure without Mary here to tell us."

"I know. But—" She showed him the photos from the envelope. The one of Mary holding baby Aleece, looking at her with such love. "Does this look like a woman who wanted to give up her child?"

Her father studied the photo, and his expression softened with sadness. "No. It doesn't."

"He said she died of a broken heart. That she never got over leaving me." She felt fresh tears fall. "What if she spent twenty-two years grieving for me while I grew up thinking she didn't want me?"

"Then that's a tragedy, but it's not your fault, and it's not your burden to carry." He pulled her back into a hug. "Whatever happened between your biological parents, whatever choices they made...you were loved. By Mary, even from a distance, and by me, every single day."

That evening, Aleece sat in her room surrounded by the photos Robert had given her. Mary looked happy in most of them, smiling, laughing, full of life. Young and in love and unprepared for what was coming. While the photos with Aleece told a different story. Mary looked older in these, worn down, scared. Like she knew what was coming and was powerless to stop it.

Aleece's phone buzzed with a text from Charles.

Thomas told me about today. Are you okay?

Instead of texting back, she called him. "I met with Robert. Learned some things and confirmed others."

"He arranged the job offer."

"Yeah. To get me to Denver so he could use me as leverage with the town council." She lay back on her bed, staring at the ceiling. "He also told me about my mother, Mary. She died three years ago."

Charles was quiet for a moment. "I'm sorry."

"The thing is, I don't think she wanted to leave me. I think Robert

CARVED IN TIMBER RIDGE

made her, and she spent the rest of her life regretting it." Her voice
broke. "Charles, what if everything I thought about my abandonment
was wrong? What if my mother loved me but couldn't keep me
because of him?"

"Then that's heartbreaking, but it doesn't change who you are, or
what you deserve now."

"I keep thinking about what you said about being with a shifter
complicating things. There's pack politics and..." Her words trailed
off. "Is that what you've been trying to protect me from? The
complications Robert was talking about?"

Another pause. "Partly."

"What else?"

"That's a conversation we need to have in person. When you're
ready." His voice was gentle. "But Aleece? Whatever complicated
things your parents had, that doesn't have to be your story. You get to
write your own ending."

After they hung up, Aleece looked at the offer letter from Sterling
and Associates. The Denver job that had seemed so appealing now
felt like a trap. A manipulation designed to get her exactly where
Robert wanted her. Whereas the county job, though, was real.
Earned on her own merit, without manipulation or ulterior motives.
The choice suddenly seemed much clearer.

Aleece pulled out her laptop and opened her email. Two
messages to write. The first one to Sterling and Associates, a thanks
but no thanks type of response. While the other one went to the
county office to accept the position. She quickly typed them up and
hit send on both before she could second-guess herself.

I'm staying in Timber Ridge.

Now she just had to tell Charles and finally have the
conversation they'd been dancing around for weeks. Whatever
complications came with being with a shifter, whatever Charles had
been trying to protect her from, she was ready to hear it.

She was ready for the truth, all of it.

CHAPTER 13
VALENTINE'S PREPARATIONS

The week after Aleece accepted the county job should have been celebratory. She'd made a decision, chosen a path, and committed to staying in Timber Ridge. Her father had been thrilled, had taken her out to dinner to celebrate, and had already started talking about helping her find her own place nearby.

But Aleece felt hollow. The morning after she'd hit send on those emails, after the relief and certainty had faded, doubt had crept in like fog. She'd accepted a job in Timber Ridge and committed to staying. But staying for what? For who?

The question that had been easy to ignore while she was making the decision now loomed large. What if staying was a mistake? What if she'd chosen Timber Ridge because of Charles, because of feelings that might not have a future? Where human-shifter relationships really were as complicated and doomed as Robert had suggested?

Her biological father's words kept echoing in her mind. *Human-shifter relationships rarely work. Your mother and I learned that the hard way.*

Now, a week before the Valentine's Festival, Aleece found

herself on a ladder in the town square, hanging string lights and drowning in uncertainty.

She'd been avoiding Charles. Had ignored his texts asking how she was doing, had made excuses when he'd suggested they get together to talk. The conversation they were supposed to have, the one where he explained everything, felt too big, too terrifying. She wasn't ready to face the complications he'd been hinting at. What if they were insurmountable? What if, like her parents, they were setting themselves up for heartbreak?

"Left side needs to be higher," Mrs. Appleton called from below. "It's drooping."

Aleece adjusted the lights mechanically, not really seeing them. The town square was being transformed for the Valentine's Festival. Red and pink decorations everywhere, heart-shaped banners, and romantic lighting. Usually, she loved this time of year, but now it just felt like a mockery. All this celebration of love when she couldn't even figure out her own heart.

"Aleece?"

She looked down to find Charles standing at the base of her ladder, work gloves in hand, concern etched on his face. Her heart did that stupid skip it always did when she saw him, which just made everything more complicated.

"Hi," she managed.

"Need help?"

"I've got it."

Charles' jaw tightened slightly. "Can we talk? When you're done?"

"I'm going to be awhile—"

"Aleece." His voice was gentle but firm. "You've been avoiding me."

She couldn't deny it, so she didn't try. "I've just been dealing with a lot."

"I know." He moved closer to the ladder. "But you don't have to deal with it alone. That's what I'm here for."

"Are you?" The words came out sharper than she had intended. "Because I don't actually know what you're here for, Charles. We've been dancing around this thing between us for weeks, but I don't know what it is or where it's going or if it can even go anywhere."

"That's what I've been trying to talk to you about."

"Well, maybe I'm not ready to talk." She climbed down the ladder, suddenly needing to be on solid ground. "Maybe I'm tired of waiting for answers that keep getting delayed. I'm starting to think there's a reason you keep putting this conversation off."

Charles looked stung. "That's not fair. I've been trying to find the right time."

"The right time? We've had dozens of right times. But there's always some reason to wait, some complication that needs explaining first." Tears filled her eyes, but she blinked them away. "I accepted the county job, I'm staying in Timber Ridge, and I did it partly... mostly because of you and whatever this is between us. But now I'm wondering if I made a huge mistake."

"Aleece—"

"Do you think humans and shifters can really build a life together?" The question burst out of her. "Can they actually make it work, or are they just setting themselves up for heartbreak?"

His whole body stilled. "Where is this coming from?"

"From reality. From what Robert told me, and from the fact that you keep warning me about complications without actually explaining what they are." She wrapped her arms around herself. "I need to know, Charles. Can this work? Can we work? Or am I deluding myself?"

"I think love is love," he said carefully, his voice measured. "I think when two people care about each other, when they're willing to put in the work, then yes, it can work. But it requires both people to choose it. To commit to it even when it's hard."

"That's not really an answer."

"It's the only answer I can give without having the full conversation first."

"Then let's have it. Right now." Her voice rose, drawing looks from other volunteers. She lowered it, but the intensity remained. "I'm done waiting, Charles. Just tell me what's so complicated that you've been putting this off for weeks."

He glanced around the town square, at the people decorating, at the very public setting. "Not here. Not like this. This conversation deserves—"

"What if there are children?" she interrupted, her fears spilling out. "What if we...if two people, human and shifter...what if they have children and the children are human? What if the shifter parent can't accept them? Can't love them because they're not shifters, too?"

The question hung in the air between them, and she saw understanding dawn in his eyes. Saw him put together what Robert must have told her, the seeds of doubt that had been planted.

"Aleece," he said slowly. "What exactly did Robert tell you?"

"The truth." She felt defensive now, protective of the fragile understanding she'd built. "That his clan wouldn't accept my mother because she was human. That they especially couldn't accept a human child. That the whole relationship was doomed from the start because she could never truly be part of his world."

"You believe him?" Charles' voice was tight.

"Why wouldn't I? He's my father. He lived it. He—"

"He forced your mother to abandon you." Charles' voice was harder now than she'd ever heard it. "They left you on the fire station steps in January, where you could have died. A father doesn't do that, Aleece. A father doesn't give up his child because of clan politics or because the child isn't what he expected. A real father fights for his child. Stays and loves them regardless."

"Like Thomas did," she whispered.

"Exactly like Thomas did." Charles took a step toward her. "Thomas raised you in a shifter community. Loved you, protected you, and gave you everything you needed. Because that's what a real parent does. What Robert did is cowardice, and using it to make you doubt what's possible between humans and shifters is manipulation."

"But what if he's right? What if there are complications we can't overcome?"

"There are always complications in relationships." He ran a hand through his hair, frustration clear. "But you don't run from them before you even understand what they are. You face them together."

"How can we face them together when you won't even tell me what they are?" she shot back. "You keep saying we need to talk, but then you never actually do. You keep warning me about complications without explaining what they are. How is that any different from what Robert did? Giving me pieces of truth but never the full picture?"

The accusation hit its mark, and she saw Charles flinch, as pain flashed across his face.

"That's not fair," he said quietly. "I've been trying to do this right. To make sure you understood everything before—"

"Before what? Before we start something? We already started something, Charles. Weeks ago. We've been building something every day I came to your house, every conversation we had, and every moment we shared." Her voice broke. "Or was I wrong about that, too? Was I imagining the connection between us?"

"You weren't imagining any of it."

"Then why are you still holding back?" Tears spilled over now, and she didn't bother wiping them away. "Why can't you just be honest with me?"

"Because I'm terrified." The words burst out of him like they'd been locked inside too long. "I'm terrified that once you know everything, once you understand what being with me means, you'll run, and I don't know if I can survive that."

The raw vulnerability in his voice stopped her anger cold. "Charles—"

"I need you to understand something about shifters," he continued, his voice steadier now. "About mates and what happens when a shifter finds the one person they're meant to be with. I need you to understand it completely, not in pieces, not standing in a town square with half of Timber Ridge watching. You deserve the full explanation, in private, where we can talk through what it means."

"Mates," she repeated. "You mean like...soulmates?"

"Something like that, but also more complicated and intense." He looked at her with such longing that she wanted to reach out and touch him. "I need you to know all of it before you decide if you want to—" He stopped. "Please, Aleece. Give me one more chance to do this right. Tonight. Come to the house tonight, and I'll tell you everything. No more delays, no more putting it off. Just the truth."

She wanted to say yes. Wanted to close the distance between them and agree to anything that would end this awful uncertainty.

But Robert's words kept echoing: *She couldn't handle my world, and I couldn't fully be in hers.*

"I don't know," she said honestly. "I don't know if I'm ready to hear whatever you need to tell me. Because what if it's exactly what I'm afraid of? What if the complications are insurmountable and we're just prolonging the inevitable?"

"Or what if they're not?" His words were gentle now. "What if I'm trying to protect you from complications that don't have to be deal-breakers, and the only thing standing between us is fear?"

"Fear based on my biological parents' experience."

"Fear based on Robert's version of events," he corrected. "Which, given everything else he's lied about, maybe shouldn't be taken as gospel. You don't have the full story, Aleece."

That stopped her. He was right. Robert had lied about the job offer, had manipulated her, and had tried to use her. Why should she trust his assessment of human-shifter relationships? But the doubt was still there, filling her thoughts.

"I just need to think," she said, stepping back from Charles. "About everything. About us, about whether I'm making decisions based on feelings that might not have a future—"

"Aleece, please don't let Robert's poison ruin what we could have." There was a desperation in Charles' voice now. "Don't let fear make your decisions for you."

"I'm not. I'm being realistic. I'm considering all the factors, including the fact that, according to Robert, my biological parents tried this and failed spectacularly." She grabbed her coat from the bench. "I need space, Charles. Time to process everything without you standing there looking at me like that."

"Like what?"

"Like I'm something precious you're about to lose." Her voice cracked. "It makes it harder to think clearly."

She walked away before he could respond, and before she could see the pain she knew would be on his face. She headed away from the town square, from the Valentine's decorations, and from the man who'd been trying so hard to do right by her.

She didn't stop until she found herself on the outskirts of town, at the trailhead where she and her father used to hike when she was younger. The winter woods were quiet, peaceful, and blessedly empty of people asking her questions or looking at her with concern.

Her phone buzzed. Thinking it might be Charles, she almost didn't pull it from her pocket, but she did. It was a message from her father.

Mrs. Appleton said you left the square upset. Are you okay?

Need some time alone. I'm fine. I'm at the trail.

Then she shoved her phone back into her coat pocket and sat on a fallen log, surrounded by silence and the skeletal remains of winter trees.

She'd made so many decisions in the past few weeks. Accepted a job. Rejected another. Confronted her biological father. Learned about her mother. But the biggest decision was whether to let herself fall completely for Charles, whether to risk her heart on something that might be as doomed as her parents' relationship, still loomed before her.

She didn't know if she were brave enough to make it. Not when the cost of being wrong felt so impossibly high. She'd spent her whole life being terrified of being unwanted, and now faced the possibility that the person she wanted most might come with complications that would tear them apart eventually anyway.

She sat in the winter woods and cried. She cried for her mother, who'd loved her but lost her, for the father who'd never fought for her, for Charles, who was trying so hard but might not be enough, and for herself, caught between the life she'd always known and a future she couldn't quite imagine.

The Valentine's Festival was a week away. A celebration of love, commitment, and forever. There she was, never more uncertain about any of it.

CHAPTER 14
THE TRUTH ABOUT
HER MOTHER

Aleece spent Saturday morning staring at the photos Robert had given her. Mary's face looked back at her from each image, young, happy, and full of hope. The woman in these photos had no idea what was coming. No idea she'd die because her heart gave out from grief and loss.

Except she was certain that Robert had lied about when Mary had died. He said it was three years ago, but Aleece had caught the way he'd hesitated, the careful adding officially into his phrasing. *Officially.* What did that mean?

She needed to know the truth. Not Robert's carefully edited version, not the story he wanted her to believe. The actual verifiable truth about what had happened to her mother. So, she went to the only person she knew who might be able to give her answers.

Shirley Winters lived in a small cottage on Oak Street, surrounded by the kind of organized chaos that comes from a lifetime of collecting information. She was Timber Ridge's unofficial historian. A bear shifter in her seventies who'd made it her life's work to document the town's history, preserve its stories, and maintain connections with other shifter communities throughout Colorado.

If anyone could find information about Mary Bran, it would be Shirley.

"Aleece!" Shirley answered the door with a warm smile, her silver hair pulled back in a neat bun. "What a lovely surprise. Come in, come in. I was just making tea."

Shirley's living room was lined floor-to-ceiling with bookshelves, filing cabinets, and boxes of documents. A large desk dominated one corner, covered in papers and what looked like genealogy charts.

"I need your help," Aleece said as Shirley bustled around making tea. "With research. I need to find out about my biological mother."

Shirley's expression grew serious. "Thomas told me your biological father showed up in town."

"Robert Way gave me some information about my mother, Mary, but I don't trust him. I need to verify what he told me. I need the truth." Aleece accepted the teacup Shirley handed her. "He said she died three years ago, but something about the way he said it felt off."

"What information do you have? Name, approximate age, location?"

"Mary Bran. If what he said is true, she would have been forty-five when she died. Robert said they were in Denver when I was born, but I don't know if that's where she was from originally."

Shirley settled into her chair with a notepad. "You were born in January 2004. This gives me a timeline to work with." She tapped her pen thoughtfully. "The Way name...that's Robert's surname?"

"Yes, but I don't know if Mary took it. I mean, I'm not sure if they were married. His clan didn't accept her. So, I don't think."

"Let me see what I can find. I have connections throughout the state, and I maintain archives of newspaper obituaries, vital records, anything that might document our community's history." Shirley stood and moved to one of her filing cabinets. "It might take a few days."

"Anything you can find, I'd appreciate it."

Shirley gave her a long look. "Aleece, honey, are you sure you want to know? Sometimes the truth is harder than uncertainty."

"I'm sure." Aleece set down her teacup. "My whole life, I've wondered why my mother gave me up. Whether she wanted me. Robert gave me answers, but I don't trust them. I need to know what really happened, even if it's painful."

"Alright then. Let me dig into my archives and make some calls." Shirley walked Aleece to the door. "I'll reach out as soon as I find something."

Aleece left with a mixture of excitement and dread. She needed to know the truth, but she wasn't certain what it would cost her.

Two days passed. Aleece threw herself into the preparations for her new job. She didn't start for another two weeks, but she needed something to distract her from thinking about Charles or Robert or the conversation she was still avoiding. Her father watched her with concern but didn't push, just kept her company and made sure she ate.

Tuesday afternoon, her phone rang, and it was Shirley.

"I found something," Shirley said without preamble. "Can you come over?"

Within minutes, Aleece was in her car, her heart pounding. The drive to Shirley's cottage was nerve-racking. It was both too long and too short. Part of her wanted to know, needed to know, while the other part of her was terrified of what she might learn.

When she pulled into the driveway, Shirley opened the door and stood in the archway. Her expression was somber, which only made Aleece more uneasy.

"Come on in, let's get out of this cold," Shirley said as Aleece got out of the car and strolled toward the porch.

Inside, laid out on the desk, as if summoning her, were several photocopied newspaper clippings and what looked like official documents.

"Sit down, honey," Shirley said gently, and Aleece's stomach dropped. Whatever she'd found, it wasn't good news.

Aleece sat, and Shirley grabbed the documents. She spread the papers out carefully.

"I found your mother's death record first," Shirley said, pulling out a form. "Mary Marie Bran died February 15, 2004. She was twenty-six years old."

The world tilted. "2004? But that would be—"

"A month and a half after you were born. One month after you were left in Timber Ridge." Shirley's voice was soft. "Robert lied to you about when she died."

Aleece stared at the date on the printout, her mind reeling. One month. Her mother had survived only one month without her.

"The official cause of death is listed as heart failure," Shirley continued, pulling out a newspaper clipping. "This is her obituary from a small paper outside Denver."

Aleece read with shaking hands:

Mary Marie Bran, 26, passed away suddenly on February 15. Born in Fort Collins, she was known for her kind heart and bright spirit. She is survived by her mother, Catherine Bran, and numerous friends. Services will be private. In lieu of flowers, donations may be made to the Children's Hospital Foundation.

No mention of Robert. No mention of a child. Like Aleece had never existed.

"There's more," Shirley said quietly. She pulled out another clipping. This one was older, from January. "I found this from when you were discovered. The fire station kept records, and this made the local paper."

The headline read: *Infant Found at Timber Ridge Fire Station.* Below was a brief description of how a baby girl had been found on the steps, bundled in blankets, with a note asking that she be cared for.

"Now look at the dates," Margaret said. "You were found on January fifteenth. Your mother died on February fifteenth. Exactly one month later, to the day."

Aleece felt cold all over. "That can't be a coincidence."

"No, honey. It's not." Shirley sat down beside her. "I've been documenting shifter communities for fifty years. I've seen this before. Not often, but often enough to recognize the pattern."

"What pattern?"

Shirley took a deep breath. "When humans bond deeply with shifters—especially when there's a mate bond involved—and then that bond is severed traumatically, it can cause physical damage. Broken heart syndrome, some doctors call it. The grief is so profound, so all-consuming, that the body literally gives up. The heart fails."

"You're saying my mother died because she gave me up?" Her voice was barely a whisper.

"I'm saying your mother died because she was separated from you. Possibly from Robert, if there was a mate bond there." Shirley's expression was filled with compassion. "The timeline suggests she tried to survive without you. Tried to go on. But the grief was too much."

Aleece felt tears spill over. "Robert said she died three years ago. He lied about when."

"He lied because the truth makes him look bad," Shirley said bluntly. "If Mary died one month after giving you up, that means his decision to force her to abandon you killed her. Maybe not directly, but the connection is clear."

"He killed her." The words came out flat, numb. "He made her give me up, and it killed her."

"Aleece—"

"All these years, I thought maybe she didn't want me. That there was something wrong with me that made her leave." Aleece's voice broke. "But she didn't want to leave. He made her, and she died from the grief of losing me."

Shirley pulled Aleece into a hug as sobs overtook her. "I'm so sorry, honey. I'm so sorry you had to learn this."

"Does my father know? About this broken heart thing?"

"I don't know. It's not common knowledge, and it doesn't happen often. Usually, only when the bond between human and shifter is especially strong." Shirley pulled back, looking at Aleece seriously. "Your mother loved you fiercely. That's what this tells me. She loved you so much that being without you literally broke her heart."

The information was too much to process. Aleece sat in Shirley's living room, surrounded by evidence of her mother's death, trying to understand.

Mary hadn't wanted to leave her. Robert had forced it, probably threatened her, manipulated her, made it impossible to stay. Mary had tried to survive, had lasted only a month before her body gave out from the grief. One month of knowing her baby was out there somewhere, being raised by strangers. The heartbreak was so profound that it had stopped her heart.

"I need to go," Aleece said abruptly, standing. "I need...I need to tell my father."

"Of course. Take the copies with you." Shirley gathered the documents into a folder. "And Aleece? Be careful with this information. Robert won't want it known that his actions led to your mother's death."

With a nod, she took the offered folder and headed to her car.

Aleece drove home on autopilot, barely seeing the road through her tears. Her hands shook on the steering wheel as the reality sank in deeper with each mile.

Her mother had loved her and had died from losing her. Robert had lied about all of it. Especially the timing, the circumstances, and probably the entire story about clan politics and impossible choices. The truth was simpler and more horrible. Robert had been a coward who'd valued his clan's standing over his family, and it had killed Mary.

Aleece pulled into the driveway and sat in her car, unable to move. The folder of documents sat on the passenger seat like evidence at a trial. Proof of love, loss, and a tragedy that could have been prevented.

Finally, she grabbed the folder and stumbled toward the house. The front door opened before she reached it. Her father must have seen her pull up.

"Aleece? What's wrong?"

She couldn't form words. Just held out the folder with shaking hands.

He took it, his expression growing grim with each page he read. When he looked up, his eyes were blazing with fury.

"He lied," her father said, his voice deadly quiet. "About everything."

"She died one month after giving me up." Her voice broke. "Shirley said it's called broken heart syndrome. She died because of losing me...because of being forced to give me up..." She couldn't finish.

Dad pulled her into a fierce hug. "I'm sorry, sweetheart. I'm so sorry."

"I spent my whole life thinking she didn't want me. That there was something wrong with me." She sobbed against his shoulder. "But she did want me. She loved me so much it killed her."

"Yes. She did." His voice was thick with emotion. "And Robert, he's going to answer for this. For lying to you, manipulating you, and for what he did to your mother."

They stood in the entryway, holding each other, while she cried for the mother she'd never known. For Mary, who'd loved her baby enough to die from losing her, and the tragedy that could have been prevented if Robert had just been brave enough to fight for his family.

Eventually, her father guided her to the sofa. "I need to call Shirley and get the details. Then—" His jaw clenched. "Then I'm going to have a conversation with Robert Way."

"What about me?" She wiped her eyes. "What am I supposed to do with this?"

"You mourn. You let yourself feel the grief, anger, and whatever else comes up." He squeezed her hand. "You remember that your mother loved you. That's what matters. Not why she had to leave, but that she never wanted to."

She looked at the documents spread on the coffee table. The death certificate with its too-soon date. The obituary that didn't mention her. The news clipping about a baby found on the fire station steps. Her mother's whole tragic story, reduced to photocopied papers.

But Shirley was right. The truth was there in the details. In the one-month gap between abandonment and death. In the heart failure diagnosis that was really grief made physical. In the date that matched exactly, like Mary had held on as long as she could before letting go.

"Charles needs to know," Aleece said suddenly. "About this and what really happened."

"Why?"

"Because—" She stopped, trying to articulate the connection forming in her mind. "Because Robert's been using my parents' relationship to make me afraid of human-shifter relationships. Saying they don't work, that complications are insurmountable, but that's not what happened. They didn't fail because humans and shifters can't make it work. They failed because Robert was a coward who chose wrong."

Understanding dawned in her father's gaze. "And you've been letting that fear influence how you see Charles."

"Yes." She stood suddenly needing to move. "I've been avoiding him because I was scared we'd end up like my biological parents. But they didn't fail because of biology, shifter politics, or any insurmountable complications. They failed because Robert gave up. When he chose his clan over his family, it destroyed them both."

"So, what are you going to do?"

156

She looked at her father, the man who'd raised her, who'd chosen her every single day for twenty-two years. Who'd shown her what real love looked like.

"I'm going to stop being a coward," she said. "I'm going to go to Charles and finally have the conversation we've been avoiding. I'm going to hear whatever complications he's been trying to warn me about, and then I'm going to decide based on facts instead of fear."

Her father smiled through his own tears. "That's my girl."

"But first..." She grabbed her phone. "First, I'm calling Robert. I'm telling him exactly what I know and where he can go with his lies and manipulations."

"Want me to do it?"

"No." Her voice was steady now, certain. "This one's mine."

She dialed Robert's number from the business card he'd given her. He answered on the second ring, his voice smooth and confident.

"Aleece. I'm glad you called. Have you thought more about my offer?"

"My mother died in February 2004," Aleece interrupted. "One month after you made her abandon me. Her heart failed from the grief of losing me. You lied about when she died and how. You lied about everything."

Silence on the other end.

"Nothing to say?" Her voice was hard. "No convenient explanation? No carefully crafted story to make yourself look better?"

"Where did you get that information?" Robert's voice had lost its smoothness.

"Does it matter? It's true, isn't it? You forced her to give me up, it killed her, and you've been lying about it ever since."

"You don't understand the circumstances—"

"I understand that you're a coward who chose his clan over his family. I understand that your choices killed my mother and cost me any chance of knowing her. Now I know that everything you've told me has been lies designed to manipulate me into doing what you want."

"Aleece, if you'd just listen—"

"No, I'm done listening to you. You're not my father. Thomas is my father. You're just the man whose cowardice destroyed my mother and gave me up like I was nothing." Aleece's voice broke, but she pushed through. "Don't contact me again. Don't come to Timber Ridge. And don't ever use my mother's memory to justify your actions. She loved me enough to die from losing me. You didn't love me enough to fight for me."

She hung up before Robert could respond.

Her father pulled her back into a hug, and she let herself cry again, for the family she never got to have. But underneath the grief was relief.

The truth, however painful, was better than the lies. And knowing her mother had loved her, that Mary's heart had literally broken from being separated from her, somehow made the abandonment hurt less. It hadn't been abandonment at all. Instead, it had been a sacrifice. Forced separation. Tragedy. But not a lack of love. Never that.

"I need to see Charles," she said when her tears finally subsided. "Tonight. I've been letting fear make my decisions, just like my mother probably did, and look where that led."

"Are you sure you're ready? You just learned—"

"I'm sure." She pulled back, wiping her eyes. "I finally understand what you've been trying to tell me all along. Real love doesn't give up when things get complicated. It fights, stays, and it chooses the person over the easy path."

"That's what Mary should have been able to do," her father said softly. "If Robert had let her."

"Yes, but I can do what she couldn't." She stood, resolve hardening. "I can choose Charles. I can face whatever complications he's been trying to warn me about, and I can fight for us instead of running away from fear."

"Then go." He nodded. "Go talk to him. Finally, have that conversation you've both been avoiding."

She grabbed her keys and the folder of documents. Charles needed to see this, needed to understand why she'd been so afraid, and why she was ready now to stop letting fear win. This move felt significant, as if she were driving toward her future rather than just to a conversation.

It was time for the truth. All of it. Starting with hers.

CHAPTER 15
CHARLES' CONFESSION

When Aleece pulled into Charles' driveway, he was already standing on the porch, waiting for her. Even in the fading light, she could see the tension in his shoulders, the concern etched on his face. Her father must have called to let Charles know she was on her way with news.

Charles came down the steps as she parked, meeting her at her car door.

"Thomas told me," he said quietly. "About your mother and what you found."

She nodded, not trusting her voice. Now that she was here, standing in front of Charles with the truth about her mother burning in her chest, she didn't know where to start.

He seemed to understand. He pulled her into a hug, solid, warm, and safe, and she let herself lean into him for a moment. Let herself take comfort from his strength.

"I'm so sorry," he murmured against her hair. "I'm so sorry you had to learn that. About Mary."

"She loved me." Her voice was muffled against his shoulder. "She died because she lost me. Her heart literally broke from grief."

"I know." His arms tightened around her. "Thomas told me everything."

They stood like that for a long moment. She drew comfort from his embrace while the winter evening darkened around them. Finally, she pulled back.

"We need to talk," she said.

"I know." He gestured toward the house. "Come inside. It's freezing out here."

The house was warm, with the fireplace crackling in the living room. He had clearly been working. Tools were scattered around, sawdust on the floor, but the space felt more finished than the last time she'd been here, more like a home.

They settled on the sofa he'd recently added, and for a moment neither spoke. The weight of everything unsaid hung between them.

"I've been afraid," she finally said. "Of ending up like my mother. Of loving a shifter and having it destroy me."

"I know." His voice was gentle. "I've been trying to give you all the information you needed to make an informed choice, but I keep putting it off because I'm terrified you'll choose to walk away."

"Then tell me now. Everything. Whatever you've been holding back."

He took a deep breath, and she saw him gathering courage. "You're my mate."

The words hung in the air between them. Her heart stuttered. "Your...what?"

"My mate. The shifter equivalent of a soulmate, but more than that. Deeper. More fundamental." He turned to face her fully. "I knew the moment I saw you, that first morning when I came to fix the pipes. The second our gazes met, my bear recognized you as my mate. The one person I'm meant to be with."

Her mind reeled. "That's real? That's an actual thing?"

"It's real. Some shifters never find their true mate. Thomas never found his. Some pair up with compatible partners, build good lives, but the mate bond..." Charles paused, searching for words. "It's different. It's recognition at a soul-deep level. Knowing with absolute certainty that this person is yours and you are theirs."

"For how long?" Her voice was barely a whisper. "You've known since the first time you saw me?"

"Since that first moment. I've been trying to find the right way to tell you ever since. Because I needed you to understand what it means before you decided anything."

"You've known for weeks." She stood abruptly, needing space. "All this time, every conversation we had, every moment we spent together...you knew I was your mate, and you didn't tell me?"

"I wanted you to have a choice." He stood too, desperation in his voice. "I didn't want you to feel trapped by biology or fate or whatever you want to call it. I wanted you to choose me because you wanted to, not because some mystical bond said you should."

"That's not your decision to make." Her voice rose. "You don't get to decide what information I need to make choices about my own life."

"I know it wasn't right, but I was terrified." He ran his hand through his hair. "The last time I thought I'd found my mate, I was wrong. Completely, devastatingly wrong."

That stopped her. "What?"

He sank back onto the sofa, and suddenly, he looked exhausted. "Seven years ago, before I moved to Timber Ridge, I met someone in Denver. A human woman named Lisa. I was so sure. The attraction was intense, the connection felt profound. I thought she was my mate."

"But she wasn't."

"No. I didn't realize that until she left me for someone else. Until she told me what we had was just physical attraction, and nothing more." His voice was hollow. "I was devastated. Thought I was broken somehow. That I'd misunderstood what the mate bond was supposed to feel like, and I'd wasted it on someone who wasn't actually mine."

"Is that why you moved here?"

"Partly. I needed to get away from Denver, from the life I'd built, expecting her to be in it. I needed to come to terms with the idea that maybe I'd never find my real mate. That maybe I'd used up my chance." He looked at her. "Then you walked into your kitchen that morning, and I knew. This was different. This was real. Everything I'd felt before was a pale imitation of this."

She sat back down slowly, trying to process. "So, what does it mean? This mate bond?"

"It means I'm irrevocably drawn to you. That my bear recognizes you as ours. That I will love you, protect you, choose you above all else for the rest of my life." His voice was raw. "It means if you choose me back, we build a life together. And if you don't..." He stopped.

"If I don't?"

"If you don't, I survive. I move on eventually. But I never find this with anyone else. You're it for me, Aleece. You're the one."

The intensity of it was overwhelming. "That's a lot of pressure to put on someone."

"I know. That's why I didn't tell you right away. I wanted you to get to know me, to care about me, if you could, without this bond hanging over everything." He reached for her hand, then pulled back. "I wanted you to choose me for me, not because biology said you should."

"But what about me? Don't I get a choice in this bond?"

"Of course you do. The mate bond isn't a guarantee of anything. It just means I recognize you as mine. You still have to choose to accept it, to build something with me. You could walk away right now, and the bond would hurt, but it wouldn't force you to stay."

She thought about her mother. About Mary, who'd loved a shifter and lost everything. "Is that what happened to my biological parents? Was there a mate bond between them?"

"I don't know. Maybe." There was a sadness in his eyes. "If there were, and if Robert forced her to give you up, that would explain why her heart literally broke. The mate bond is powerful. Severing it traumatically can be...devastating."

"So, you're saying if I accept this bond, if I choose you, and then something happens...like if we're forced apart, I could die?" The fear in her voice was clear.

"No." He scooted closer, his voice urgent. "Not if it's your choice to leave. The broken heart syndrome Shirley told you about happens when the bond is severed against someone's will. When they're forced away from their mate, when they have no choice. If you chose to leave me, it would hurt, but it wouldn't kill either of us."

"But my mother..."

"Your mother didn't choose to leave you or Robert. She was forced. That's the difference." Charles took her hand and held it gently. "I would never force you to do anything, Aleece. I would never demand you stay, or manipulate you, or use the mate bond to control you. You have all the power here. All the choice."

She looked at their joined hands, trying to organize her swirling thoughts. "You said your bear recognizes me. What does that mean exactly?"

"It means the animal part of me, you could call it my shifter instincts, knows you're mine. My bear calms around you in a way it never does otherwise. Protective. Possessive, honestly, though I try to keep that in check." He smiled slightly. "It's why I had such a hard time controlling myself around you. It was why I kept pulling away when we got close. My bear wanted to claim you immediately, but I knew you needed time."

"Claim me how?"

"Kiss you. Mark you as mine. Make it clear to every other male that you're mine." He cleared his throat. "But again, I didn't want to pressure you or make you feel like you had to accept this just because my instincts are screaming that you're my mate."

"This is insane." She pulled her hand back, standing again. "You're telling me that some mystical bond decided we're meant to be together, and I just have to what? Accept it? Build my life around it?"

"No. You decide what we've built together. The friendship, connection, and feelings developed naturally. That wasn't some bond." He stood too, maintaining a distance this time. "The mate bond just explains why I fell so hard so fast. But what you feel, whether you want to be with me or not, that has to come from you. From *your* choice."

"I don't know what I feel." Her voice broke. "I thought I was falling for you naturally. But now I don't know if what I felt was real or just some biological response to your mate bond thing."

"It's real." His voice was certain. "The mate bond doesn't make you feel things, Aleece. It just means I recognize you. What you feel is all you. Your emotions, your choices, and your connection to me."

She wrapped her arms around herself, feeling overwhelmed. "I need to think. I need to process all of this."

"I understand."

"My mother died, Charles. Her heart broke from losing me, from losing Robert, from being forced away from her family. I don't understand it all, but that's what Shirley said. Now, you're asking me to risk the same thing."

"I'm not asking you to risk anything." He moved closer, his voice desperate now. "I'm telling you that I love you. That I'm in love with you. That I have been since that first day, and I will be for the rest of my life, whether you choose me or not."

The words should have been romantic. They should have made her heart soar. Instead, they just added to the weight pressing down on her chest.

"You love me." She felt tears prick her eyes. "You love me, and there's this mate bond, and you've been keeping all of this from me for weeks while I fell for you, not knowing any of it."

"I was trying to do the right thing—"

"By lying? By withholding information?" She hollered. "You were so worried about me having a choice, but you took away my ability to make an informed choice by not telling me the truth."

"You're right." His shoulders slumped. "You're absolutely right. I should have told you sooner. Should have been honest from the start instead of trying to protect you from information you deserved to have."

"Yes, you should have." She grabbed her jacket. "You should have told me the first day, or the second, or any of the dozens of days I spent here helping you build your house, thinking I was helping a friend."

"Aleece, please don't leave like this—"

"I need time, Charles. I need space to figure out what I think about all of this without you standing there looking at me like—" Her voice cracked. "Like I'm your everything when I don't even know if I can be."

"You don't have to be anything. You just have to be you." His voice was thick with emotion. "That's all I've ever wanted."

"I'm scared." The admission came out small, broken. "I'm scared of ending up like my mother. Loving someone so much that losing them destroys me. Of giving my heart completely and having it used against me like Robert used Mary's love."

"I'm not Robert." His voice was firm despite the pain in his eyes. "I would never force you to choose between me and anything else. I would never manipulate you or use your feelings against you. And I would never, ever abandon our children no matter what."

"You say that now—"

"I say it *always*." He closed the distance between them, cupping her face gently. "Listen to me, Aleece. I love you. The mate bond told me you were mine, but I fell in love with you. Watching you learn to use a circular saw. Listening to you talk about feeling torn between worlds and seeing you throw yourself into building something even though you had no experience. The bond just gave me the certainty that what I felt was real and permanent. The rest is all us."

Tears spilled over, and he wiped them away with his thumbs. "I don't want to lose you," she whispered. "But I'm terrified of what keeping you might cost."

"I know. I can't promise it won't be complicated. There will be shifter politics, questions about children, and integration into shifter society. All the things Robert probably told you about and more. Most of it will be from outside Timber Ridge than within our community. But none of it is insurmountable. None of it is worth losing what we could have together."

She pulled back from his touch. "I need time. I need to think about all of this without you here, making me want to—" She stopped herself.

"Want to what?"

"Stay. Choose you. Say yes to everything, even though I'm terrified." She moved toward the door. "I need to figure out if I'm brave enough for this. If I can risk my heart the way my mother did and hope for a different ending."

"Take all the time you need. I'll be here. Waiting. However long it takes."

She grabbed the doorknob and then turned back. He stood in the middle of his living room, in the house he'd built with the hope she might share it with him, looking like his heart was breaking. "Charles?"

"Yeah?"

"You should have told me. From the beginning. You should have trusted me with the truth instead of trying to protect me from it."

"I know. I'm sorry. I'm so sorry, Aleece."

She left before she could change her mind, before she could cross the room and kiss him and choose him despite her fears. The cold night air hit her like a slap, and she hurried to her car with tears streaming down her face.

In her rearview mirror, she could see Charles standing in the doorway, backlit by the warm glow of the house, watching her leave. Not following, not chasing, just letting her go because he'd promised her the choice. Somehow, that made it hurt worse.

She drove down the winding driveway, watching him disappear in her mirror, and felt like her own heart was breaking. Just like she'd been so afraid would happen.

But she kept driving. Kept putting distance between herself and the man who loved her, who'd been trying so hard to do right by her that he'd done everything wrong. She kept driving because she was too scared to turn back. Too afraid to trust that their ending could be different from Robert and Mary's. In that moment, she was too scared to be brave.

By the time she got home, she was sobbing so hard she could barely see. Her father was waiting on the porch, and he pulled her into his arms without a word, letting her cry against his shoulder while the winter night deepened around them.

"I love him," she gasped between sobs. "I love him, but I'm scared to choose him."

"I know, sweetheart. I know."

"Mary loved Robert, and it killed her."

"Your mother loved you, too. That love was real, beautiful, and worth everything, even the tragedy." He pulled back, looking at her seriously. "But you're not your mother, and Charles isn't Robert. You get to write your own story."

"What if I write it wrong? What if I choose him and it ends the same way?"

"What if you don't choose him and spend the rest of your life wondering what if?" he countered gently. "Fear is a terrible reason to turn away from love, Aleece."

Yet, she couldn't shake the terrifying certainty that history was repeating itself, and she was too afraid to stop it.

CHAPTER 16
A FATHER'S WISDOM

T wo days before the Valentine's Festival, Aleece woke before dawn and couldn't fall back asleep. She'd barely slept since leaving Charles' house. Every time she closed her eyes, she saw him standing in that doorway, watching her drive away.

She made coffee and curled up in the window seat, watching the sun rise over Timber Ridge. The town was peaceful in the early morning light, snow-covered and quiet. Beautiful. Home. But all she could think about was Charles, likely alone in his house in the woods, building a life he'd hoped to share with her.

"You're up early."

She turned to find her father in the doorway, already dressed, with two coffee mugs in his hands. His expression was determined in a way that made her stomach clench.

"Couldn't sleep," she said.

"Neither could I." He handed her a fresh mug and sat down across from her. "We need to talk."

"Dad, if this is about Charles—"

"It's about Mary." His voice was gentle but firm. "And about the conclusions you've been drawing from what happened to her."

She wrapped her hands around the warm mug. "I know what happened. She loved Robert. He forced her to give me up, and she died from the grief. Her heart literally broke."

"That's true, but you're missing something crucial." He leaned forward. "After you told me what Shirley found, I did some more digging. Called in some favors, talked to people who knew Mary, and looked into the timeline more carefully."

"What did you find?"

"Mary didn't die because she loved a shifter, Aleece. She died because she was separated from her child." Her father held her gaze. "The timeline proves it. Robert or his clan forced Mary to leave him months before you were born. He'd convinced her that if she gave you up, she'd be welcomed back. They'd been separated before you were born, according to people who knew them. She was handling that. She might have wanted to be with him, or maybe she didn't think she could give you what you deserved, but when she had to give you up days later, that's what killed her."

"But Robert said—"

"Robert has been lying about everything to suit his narrative." Her father's voice hardened. "He's been making you think human-shifter relationships are doomed, that complications are insurmountable. But that's not what destroyed your parents. Robert destroyed them. His cowardice, his choices, and his refusal to fight for his family."

"I know he's a coward. I know he chose wrong—"

"But you've been letting his failures shape your fears about Charles." Her father set down his coffee. "Sweetheart, your mother's heart broke because she lost you. Not because she loved a shifter, shifter politics, or any of the things Robert wants you to believe. She died because Robert forced her to give up her daughter, and that loss was more than she could survive."

The words hit her like a physical blow. "She died because of me."

"No." He shook his head. "She died because of Robert. Because he demanded she choose between you and him, and when she chose you by trying to give you a better life even though it was killing her, he didn't fight for any of you. He let her go. He let you go. And that killed her."

Tears streamed down her face. "I don't understand. Why are you telling me this?"

"Because you're making the same mistake she did." He reached across and took her hand. "You're letting fear make your decisions. You're choosing to protect yourself from potential pain instead of fighting for who you love. I won't watch you do that to yourself. I won't watch you walk away from Charles because you're afraid of becoming your mother when the real risk is becoming Robert."

"What?"

"Robert was the one who ran. He chose fear over love. He decided that the approval of the clan was worth more than his family." Her father squeezed her hand. "Don't be like him, Aleece. Be like your mother, brave enough to love even when it's scary, but be smarter than she was. Don't let anyone force you to choose between the person you love and the life you want."

"Charles wouldn't do that—"

"I know he wouldn't. That's my point." He nodded. "Charles is giving you the choice Robert never gave Mary. He's being honest about what a life with him means, letting you decide if you can handle it, respecting your autonomy even when it's killing him. That's not Robert. That's the opposite of Robert."

She pulled her hand back, wrapping her arms around herself. "But what if I'm not strong enough? What if I choose him and then something happens—"

"Something will happen. Life is full of somethings." Her father stood and moved to look out the window. "You could choose Charles and face complications with shifter politics. But look at Nico, the alpha of Timber Ridge, his mate is human. Or you could choose to stay safe and spend the rest of your life wondering what if. Here's what I know: you're miserable without him. You've been miserable since you left his house two days ago."

"I'm scared."

"I know, and that's okay." He turned back to face her. "But let me tell you something about your mother. About Mary. I never met her, but I've read everything Shirley could find. I've talked to people who knew her. And you know what I learned?"

"What?"

"She was brave. She was so, so brave." The emotion was thick in his voice. "She loved you fiercely from the moment you were born. And when Robert demanded she give you up, she didn't just abandon you. She researched towns, found the safest place for a human-shifter child to be raised by shifters, made sure you'd be found immediately, and bundled you in warm blankets even though it was breaking her heart. She gave you the best chance she could, even though it killed her."

"Why are you telling me this?"

"Because you have her courage in you. Her capacity to love and her strength." He sat back down beside her. "You also have choices she didn't have. Charles isn't demanding you give up anything. He's offering you everything. The only thing stopping you from accepting is fear."

"Dad—"

"I need to tell you something else, about Robert." He slid his phone out of his pocket and pulled up a document. "I've been doing more research into Way Enterprises and into Robert's business dealings."

She took the phone, scrolling through what looked like planning proposals and council meeting minutes. "What am I looking at?"

"Robert's been trying to develop property in Timber Ridge for three years. He wants to build a resort complex near the state park. Something that would significantly change the character of our town. The council has rejected his proposals repeatedly because his plans don't respect the community's values or environmental concerns."

"He said something about wanting to build something here. But what does that have to do with me?" Understanding clicked.

"He thought having a daughter *from* Timber Ridge would give him leverage. That maybe I'd be more sympathetic to his proposals if he could claim family ties." Her father's expression grew grim. "That job offer he arranged? It wasn't just about getting you to Denver. It was about getting you away from here so you couldn't see what he was really doing. So, you couldn't warn the council or me about his manipulations."

Her stomach churned. She'd realized he was trying to use her, but she hadn't realized the depth of his deception. "He wasn't trying to have a relationship with me at all."

"I think part of him wanted that. Probably felt some guilt about Mary and about you, but his primary motivation was business. Access." Her father took back his phone. "He's been using you from the moment he showed up in Timber Ridge. The sob story about your mother, the job offer, even the lies about when she died. All calculated to manipulate you into doing what he wanted."

"I should have seen it."

"How could you? You were vulnerable, wanting answers about your biological parents. He exploited that. But now you know. Now you can make decisions based on the truth instead of his manipulations."

She stood, pacing to the window. Outside Timber Ridge was waking up. Lights coming on in houses, people starting their days. Her home. The place she'd chosen to stay.

"Charles isn't like Robert," she said quietly.

"No, he's not."

"He's been trying to give me choices, information, and power."

"Yes."

"And I've been punishing him for it. For not telling me about the mate bond immediately, when really, he was just trying to do right by me." She spun toward her father. "I've been so afraid of ending up like my mother that I didn't see. I'm not her. Charles isn't Robert. We get to write our own story."

"Yes, you do." He smiled. "So, what story do you want to write?"

She thought about Charles standing in his doorway, watching her leave, and about the way he looked at her like she was everything, but still stepped back and gave her space to choose. She also considered the mate bond that meant he would love her forever, but didn't force her to love him back.

"I want to write a story where I'm brave," she said. "Where I don't let fear win. Instead, I choose love even though it's terrifying."

"Then you know what you need to do."

She grabbed her phone, then stopped. "What if he's changed his mind? What if my leaving was too much?"

"That man built you a house, Aleece. A whole house. With a master bedroom that catches the sunrise and a deck with the perfect view, and every detail chosen with you in mind." Her father stood, pulling her into a hug. "He's not going to change his mind just because you needed time to process. He said he'd wait, and he will."

"How do you know?"

"Because that's what you do when you really love someone. You wait. You give them space, and you trust they'll come back when they're ready." He leaned back, looking at her seriously. "I think you're ready now, aren't you?"

"I'm ready," she said. "I'm terrified, but I'm ready."

"Good." He kissed her forehead. "Then go. The Valentine's Festival is in two days, but don't wait. Go now, tell him how you feel, stop running from the best thing that's ever happened to you."

"What do I say?"

"The truth. That you love him. That you chose him, and you're done letting fear make your decisions. Then maybe apologize for being scared and for making him wait so long. But also warn him you're always stubborn." Her father smirked at her.

She laughed despite her tears. "I can do that."

"I know you can. You're Mary's daughter. Brave, fierce, and full of love. But you're also my daughter, which means you're smart enough to learn from other people's mistakes instead of repeating them."

"Dad—" Her voice broke. "Thank you for everything. For raising me and loving me as you do, and most of all for not giving up on me even when I was being impossible."

"That's what real fathers do." His brows furrowed. "Charles will be that kind of father, too, if you two decide to have children, because he's nothing like Robert. Nothing."

"They'll have two strong, powerful, and protective males in their lives." She hugged him tight.

"I'm going to see him," she said, pulling back. "Right now. Before I lose my nerve."

"Go." He pushed her gently toward the stairs. "Get dressed, make yourself presentable, and go get your mate."

The word *mate* no longer felt frightening. Rather, it felt right, as if meant to be.

She rushed upstairs, threw on clothes, and ran a brush through her hair. She looked down at her jeans and sweater and decided they'd have to do, because she couldn't wait another minute.

In the mirror, she caught a glimpse of herself—eyes bright with tears and determination, cheeks flushed, looking more alive than she had in days. She looked like someone brave enough to choose love and someone ready to fight for her happy ending instead of running from it. Like Mary's daughter, finally making the choice her mother should have been able to make.

Aleece ran downstairs, pausing only to hug Thomas one more time.

"I'm proud of you," he said. "So proud."

"I haven't done anything yet."

"Yes, you have. You chose courage over fear. Everything else is just details."

"Love you, Dad." She smiled at him and ran out the door.

"Love you too, sweetheart."

The sun was fully up now, painting the snow-covered landscape in shades of gold and pink. Beautiful. Like the world was celebrating her choice. As she drove toward Charles, she practiced what she'd say. Every rehearsed speech felt inadequate, too small for the enormity of what she felt.

Charles' driveway came into view, and she spotted his truck there, smoke rising from the chimney. He was there.

She parked and sat for a moment, gathering courage. Through the window, she could see Charles, probably making coffee, starting his day without her. That was about to change. She got out of the car and walked toward the house, toward Charles and the future she was finally brave enough to choose.

The front door opened before she reached it. Charles stood in the doorway, surprise and hope warring on his face.

"Aleece?"

"I need to tell you something," she said, her voice shaking but steady. "I need to tell you that I've been an idiot, and I'm sorry, and I'm ready now. I'm ready to hear everything, to face whatever complications come with choosing you, to write our own story instead of being afraid of repeating my parents' mistakes."

He stepped onto the porch, his expression transforming. "You're sure?"

"I'm terrified, but I'm sure." She stepped closer. "I realized something. My mother didn't die from loving a shifter. She died from losing me. The tragedy wasn't the relationship. It was being forced to choose. You're not forcing me to choose anything. You're giving me every choice. Every piece of information and every opportunity to walk away."

"And you're not walking away?" His voice was rough with emotion.

"No, I'm done running." She closed the last bit of distance between them and looked up at the man, who'd been so patient, careful, and determined to do right by her. "I'm choosing you, Charles. I'm choosing us. I'm going to be brave, like my mother should have been able to be."

He pulled her into his arms, and the tightness in her shoulders melted away. This was home. Where she was supposed to be. Not just the house, not just Timber Ridge, but with him.

"I love you," she whispered against his chest. "I think I have since that first day, I was just too scared to admit it."

"I love you too." His arms tightened around her. "I love you so much, Aleece. I promise I will never make you choose between me and anything else. I will choose you every single day for the rest of our lives."

"I know." And she did know. Finally, completely. "That's why I'm here. That's why I'm staying."

They stood on the porch, holding each other while the morning brightened around them, and the last of her fear dissolved.

This was the story she was meant to write. Unlike her mother's story, this one would have a happy ending.

CHAPTER 17
VALENTINE'S EVE

Aleece woke on the morning of Valentine's Eve, tangled in Charles' sheets, sunlight streaming through the master bedroom windows. For a moment, she just lay there, watching the golden light dance through the curtain, while listening to Charles' steady breathing beside her.

They'd spent the previous day talking. She now understood how the mate bond truly worked and what it meant. They'd discussed that if they had children, they had a fifty-fifty chance of them being a shifter. All the things Robert had made sound insurmountable, Charles made sound like challenges they could face together. Somewhere around midnight, exhausted and emotionally wrung out but happier than she'd been in weeks, she had fallen asleep in Charles' arms.

Now, watching him sleep, his face relaxed, the usual tension gone, she felt certain. This was right. This was home.

Her phone buzzed on the nightstand. Robert.

She slipped out of bed carefully, not wanting to wake Charles. She grabbed her cell phone and stepped out onto the deck they'd built together to take the call.

"What do you want?" she answered, her voice cold.

"Aleece. I was hoping we could talk—"

"No." The word was firm. "I know everything now. About when my mother really died, your development deals, and why you really showed up in Timber Ridge."

Silence on the other end.

"You used me," she continued. "You used my mother's memory, my need for answers, everything, to try to manipulate me into helping your business interests. I'm done. Stay away from me, my family, and from Timber Ridge."

"You don't understand the full picture."

"I understand that you're a coward who killed my mother with your choices and then lied about it for twenty years." Her voice shook, but she stayed strong. "I understand that you tried to manipulate me into repeating her mistakes, and that you're nothing like the father who actually raised me."

"Aleece, if you'd just listen—"

"No," she snapped. "I'm done listening to you. Don't call me again. Don't contact Thomas. Don't come to Timber Ridge. We're done."

She hung up before Robert could respond, then blocked his number. Her hands were shaking, but she felt lighter. Freer. As she closed that chapter of her life, permanently.

"Everything okay?"

She turned to find Charles in the doorway, bare-chested, hair rumpled from sleep, concern on his face.

"It is now." She moved back inside, into his arms. "That was Robert. I told him to leave us alone."

"How do you feel?"

"Good. Really good." She pulled back to look at him. "I don't need him. I never did. I have Thomas and you. That's all the family I need."

He kissed her forehead. "What do you want to do today?"

"I have an idea." She grabbed her phone. "But I need to make a stop first."

An hour later, they pulled into the hardware store parking lot in Charles' truck. Aleece had a list, and Charles was looking at her with bemused curiosity.

"What exactly are we building?" he asked as she loaded lumber into the truck bed.

"You'll see." She added paint, brushes, and sandpaper. "Trust me."

They drove back to Charles' house, and she led him upstairs to the guest bedroom, the one they'd been working on together before everything had fallen apart.

He stopped in the doorway, his expression, his gaze darkened, and his brows knitted together. The room was partially demolished, baseboards torn up, and walls damaged in places. It looked like someone had taken their grief out on the space.

"I came here after you left," he said quietly. "After you said you needed time to think. I couldn't stand looking at the work we'd done together. So, I..." He gestured helplessly at the damage.

"I know." She set down her supplies. "Dad told me. He said he stopped by the next morning and saw the damage. Now we're fixing it. Together. Today."

"Aleece—"

"No arguments. We're going to make this room beautiful again. Better than before." She handed him a pry bar. "Because that's what we do. We build and fix things. We make broken things whole."

"You're talking about more than the room."

"I'm talking about us. About how we took something beautiful, almost broke it completely, and now we're going to put it back together stronger than before."

They worked side by side. Repairing the damaged drywall, installing new baseboards, and sanding rough edges smooth. The physical labor was cathartic, each hammer strike and brush stroke an affirmation: *We're building this together. We're choosing this together.*

Around one, they broke for lunch—sandwiches eaten sitting on the subfloor, shoulders touching, comfortable in the silence.

"Thank you," he said finally. "For coming back and giving us another chance."

"Thank you for waiting." She leaned against him. "For not giving up on me even when I was being stubborn and scared."

"I would have waited forever." His voice was simple, certain. "That's what you do when you love someone."

They finished the room as the sun began to set. Fresh paint on the walls, a warm gray that she'd chosen. New trim around the windows, and the floor refinished until it was gleaming. It looked better than before. More intentional. More *them.*

"It's perfect," he said, surveying their work.

"Not quite." She pulled out her phone, scrolling to a photo she'd taken weeks ago. "Remember this? When we first looked at this room?"

It was a picture of the space before they'd started work. Damaged, neglected, full of potential.

"Yeah. It needed so much work."

"But you could see what it would become. You had the vision even when it looked hopeless." She looked around the finished room. "That's how I feel about us. Even when things looked impossible, even when I was running scared, you could see what we could be, and you were right."

He pulled her close, and they stood together in the center of the room they'd destroyed and rebuilt. A metaphor for what they'd done with their relationship.

"What happens now?" she asked.

"Now?" His voice was warm. "Now we go to the Valentine's Festival tomorrow. We dance in the town square, eat too much chocolate, and let everyone in Timber Ridge see that we're together, really together, and we don't care who knows it."

"And after?"

"After, we keep building. This house, our life, our future." He turned her to face him. "But one step at a time. Today we fixed a room. Tomorrow, we celebrate. The day after that, we figure out the next thing."

"I like that plan." She reached up and placed her hand on his cheek. "One step at a time."

I made a different choice. I chose to be brave and to fight, and because of that, I got a different ending.

"What are you thinking about?" he asked.

"Mary." She traced her fingers along the curve of his jaw. "Wishing she could have had this. This chance at happiness with someone who chose her back."

"She gave you that chance, though. By making sure you ended up somewhere safe, somewhere you could thrive." He pulled her closer. "She chose you, Aleece. Even when it cost her everything."

"I know. I'm going to honor that choice by living fully. By being brave enough to love you without fear."

"No fear?"

"Well, some fear. Change is scary, and the future is uncertain." She smiled up at him. "But the fear doesn't get to win anymore. Love wins. We win."

"We win," he echoed and kissed the top of her head.

CHAPTER 18
CLAIMING THEIR FUTURE

For the second morning in a row, Aleece woke in Charles' arms. This is what she wanted to wake up to every morning. She twisted toward him to find him watching her.

"Good morning," Charles murmured against her hair.

"Good morning." She studied his features in the soft light. "Before we go to the festival today, there's something we need to do."

He cocked an eyebrow at her. "What's that?"

"The claiming. The mate bond." Her heart was pounding, but her voice was steady. "You said when shifters find their mates, there's a claiming. A way to make the bond official, to let everyone know you've chosen each other."

"Aleece..." His voice was rough. "Are you sure? Once we complete the bond, there's no going back. Everyone will know. Every shifter in town will sense it."

"That's exactly what I want." She sat up, pulling the sheet around her. "I want everyone to know we've made our choice. That we've chosen each other completely. I don't want there to be any doubt, any speculation, any room for people like Robert to try to come between us."

187

He sat up too, his dark eyes searching hers. "You understand what you're asking? The bond is permanent. It's a commitment that goes deeper than marriage, deeper than any human tradition. It ties our souls together."

"I know." She reached out and took his hand in hers. "Shirley explained it to me. How shifters mark their mates, how the bond becomes visible to other shifters, how it changes everything. I want that. I want everyone in Timber Ridge to look at us today at the festival and know we've claimed our future. We're mated forever."

"Forever," he repeated, his voice thick with emotion. "You're choosing forever with me."

"Yes." She moved closer, cupping his face. "I'm choosing you, Charles Monroe. I'm choosing this bond and this life. I'm choosing it all, completely, with my whole heart."

He closed his eyes, and when he opened them again, they were blazing with golden light. His bear rose to the surface. "You have no idea how long I've wanted to hear you say that."

"Then claim me." Her voice was steady despite her racing heart. "Before we go to the festival, before we face everyone, make me yours, Charles. Let the bond complete. Let everyone know I'm your mate and you're mine."

"Aleece—" His hands trembled as they framed her face. "Are you absolutely certain? Because once I start, once my bear recognizes that you're accepting the bond, I won't be able to stop. I won't want to stop."

"I don't want you to stop." She leaned into him. "I want you. Forever."

The word *forever* seemed to snap something in him. He pulled her to him with a desperate sound that reminded her of a mixture of a moan and a growl, and his lips crashed against hers.

This kiss was different from the ones before. Deeper. More urgent. More *claiming*.

She felt heat flood through her, starting at her lips and spreading outward. His hands were in her hair, on her back, pulling her impossibly closer. She could feel his bear just beneath the surface and sense the animal's possessive joy at her finally accepting the bond.

"Mine," he growled against her lips, and the word resonated through her entire body.

"Yours," she agreed, and felt something inside her chest *click* into place.

The mate bond.

It was like a door she hadn't known existed suddenly opening, connecting her heart directly to his. She could feel him. Not his thoughts exactly, but his emotions. The overwhelming love, fierce protectiveness, and the soul-deep satisfaction of having his mate finally accept him.

"I feel you," she gasped. "Charles, I can feel you inside me—"

"The bond," he said roughly, pulling back to look at her. His eyes were still glowing gold. "It's starting to form. But we need to complete it. I need to—" He stopped, seeming to struggle for control. "I need to mark you. To make it permanent."

"Then do it." She pulled him back to her. "Claim me, Charles. Make me yours in every way that matters."

He groaned and kissed her again, deeper this time. His hands moved over her body with reverent desperation—learning, claiming, marking. Every touch sent sparks through the bond forming between them, until she felt like she was drowning in sensation.

When his lips moved to her neck, she tilted her head instinctively, offering herself. He hesitated, his breath hot against her skin.

"This will hurt for just a moment," he warned. "The claiming bite. It's how shifters mark their mates. It leaves a permanent mark that other shifters can see."

"I want it." Her voice was steady. "I want everyone to know I'm yours."

His teeth scraped against her neck, and then pressure, sharp and intense. She gasped as she felt his teeth break skin, felt him mark her.

But the pain was fleeting, immediately replaced by a rush of sensation so powerful it stole her breath.

The mate bond, which had been forming gradually, suddenly snapped fully into place.

She felt everything. Charles' love, his devotion, his absolute certainty that she was his, and he was hers. She felt his bear's possessive satisfaction, his human heart's overwhelming joy, and the way every cell in his body recognized her as *mate*. Underneath it all, she felt herself settling. Like pieces of her that had always been restless and uncertain, finally finding their proper place. Like coming home after a lifetime of wandering.

"Charles," she breathed, and his name felt different now. More significant. Because he wasn't just the man she loved, he was her mate. Her other half. Her forever.

"I've got you." He pulled back from her neck, licking the mark he'd made. She felt the wound tingle and knew it was already beginning to heal. Shifter saliva had properties that helped their mates recover from the claiming bite. "I've got you, mate, my everything."

He laid her back on the bed, and their bodies came together with a rightness that made her want to weep. Every touch, every kiss, every movement was amplified through the bond. She could feel his pleasure as well as her own, could sense his desperate love, his fierce protectiveness, and his absolute certainty that this was right.

"I love you," she gasped as sensation built. "I love you so much."

"I love you," his voice was rough against her ear. "My mate. My heart. My home."

The claiming was emotional, passionate, and tender all at once. He moved over her with reverent desperation, whispering words in a language she didn't understand. Something old and primal that his bear was speaking through him. Promises, vows, claims of possession and devotion.

Through the bond, she could feel everything he felt. The overwhelming relief that she'd finally chosen him, the fierce joy of claiming his mate, and the soul-deep satisfaction of being complete at last. She sent him her own feelings back. Her love, trust, and absolute certainty that she'd made the right choice.

When they finally reached completion together, the bond between them flared brilliant and permanent. She felt it settle into her chest, warm, right, and forever.

She was claimed. Mated. His. Just as he was hers.

They lay tangled together afterward, both trembling with emotion and exhaustion. His hand was over the mark on her neck. A possessive gesture that his bear clearly needed. She could feel through the bond how important it was to him, this visible sign that she belonged to him.

"How does it feel?" he asked quietly. "The bond?"

She considered trying to find words for something so profound. "Like I was incomplete before and didn't know it. Now I'm whole." She turned to look at him. "I can feel you. Inside me. Your emotions, your presence, it's like you're part of me now."

"That's exactly what it is." He kissed her forehead. "We're bound together now, Aleece. Soul-deep. Forever."

"Forever," she repeated, and the word didn't scare her anymore. It felt right. Perfect.

She gently touched the mark on her neck, feeling the raised edges. "What does it look like?"

"Beautiful." His voice was thick with emotion. "It looks like two halves joining together. Like roots intertwining. It's unmistakably a claiming mark. Every shifter who sees it will know you're mated."

"Good." She smiled. "Let them know. Let everyone know."

They lay quietly for a while, adjusting to the bond. She could feel his presence in her mind, not intrusive, just *there*. Comforting. Right. Like having a constant connection to home.

"I can feel your emotions," she said wonderingly. "Right now, you're happy. Content. A little bit smug."

He laughed. "Smug?"

"Very smug. Your bear is basically preening that you've finally claimed your mate."

"Can you blame him? I've waited months for this." He pulled her closer. "Sure, I'm smug, happy, and so deeply in love with you that I can barely think straight."

She could feel the truth of his words through the bond. The overwhelming love, the bone-deep satisfaction, the certainty that she was his, and he was hers forever.

"I love you too," she whispered. "My mate. My home. My everything."

He kissed her again, soft and reverent this time. "We should probably get up soon. The festival starts at noon, and everyone will be wondering where we are."

"Let them wonder." She snuggled closer. "I want a few more minutes of just us before we share this with the world."

"A few more minutes," he agreed, wrapping his arms around her.

They lay together as the sun rose fully, painting the room in golden light. The house they'd built together, the life they were creating, it all felt perfect now. Complete. Through the windows, she could see the deck they'd built, the forest beyond with the mountains rising in layers of blue and gray. Beautiful. Home. But the most beautiful thing was the man beside her, connected to her now in a way that could never be broken. Her mate, her forever.

"Okay," she finally said, pulling back reluctantly. "We should get ready. I want to show everyone my claiming mark, and I want them all to know we've chosen each other."

"Are you sure?" His hand traced over the mark on her neck. "There might be talk."

"Let them talk. Let them speculate." She sat up, feeling powerful and claimed and ready to face the world. "I don't care what anyone thinks. I chose you, you chose me, and that's all that matters."

His eyes blazed gold again, his bear responding to her certainty. "You're incredible. You know that?"

"I'm yours. That's what I am." She leaned down to kiss him.

"Now come on. Let's get ready to tell Timber Ridge that their handyman has finally found his mate."

The Valentine's Festival awaited, full of celebration, community, and love. But the real celebration had already happened here, in this house in the woods, when two people brave enough to choose each other had completed a bond that would last forever.

Mine, Charles' bear whispered through the bond.

Ours, Aleece, corrected, and felt his joy at the word.

Not his alone. Not hers alone.

Theirs. Together. Forever.

Exactly as it was always meant to be.

PREVIEW: RETURN TO TIMBER RIDGE

Coming October 2026

S he ran from control. He ran from pain. Together, they'll learn that home is worth the risk.
Lucia Matthews left Timber Ridge at eighteen and never looked back. As a corporate lawyer weeks from making partner, she's built a life on one principle: never let anyone control you again. Until her pregnant sister-in-law's crisis pulls her home and she meets Kory.

Kory Denton is a man with ghosts. Following the death of his mate, he's been on the run and never looked back. After Christmas, he's gone. That's the plan.

But the mate bond has other ideas. An unexpected stay on a Christmas tree farm ignites something neither can ignore. Lucia's life crumbles as she's forced to choose between partnership or presence, career or connection. Kory's walls crack when a stubborn lawyer refuses to let him push her away.

Between a law firm demanding everything, a seven-year-old who needs her mother, and a broken shifter ready to heal, Lucia must decide what she's really running toward. Kory must decide if he's brave enough to stop running and start living.

CHAPTER ONE:
THE WEEKLY DRIVE

The Denver skyline was disappearing in Lucia's rearview mirror when her phone rang. The dashboard lit up, displaying the last name she wanted to see right now, *Richard*.

"Of course."

Technically off the clock, Lucia considered letting it go to voicemail, but associates who wanted to make partner didn't ignore senior partners. Even on Friday afternoons, when they were an hour into a six-hour drive.

"Lucia Matthews," she answered, keeping her voice professional despite her annoyance.

"Where are you?" Richard Nickles' tone was clipped, impatient. "I called your office, and your assistant said you'd left already."

"I'm heading to Timber Ridge for the weekend for a family visit. I mentioned it in Monday's meeting."

"Right...your brother." There was a pause, loaded with disapproval. "Third weekend this month."

"Second," Lucia corrected, though she knew it wouldn't matter.

She merged onto the highway, heading into the mountains. "I'll have my laptop, if something urgent comes up."

"The Cannon's case *is* urgent. Depositions start next week, and we're not ready."

Lucia bit back a response. They were absolutely ready. She'd spent the past two weeks preparing. Every document was organized, and every witness was prepared, but Richard didn't like to be contradicted, even when he was wrong.

"I'll review the files again this weekend," she said instead. "If you need me to come back Sunday night instead of Monday morning—"

"What I need is for you to be in the office. Present and committed." His voice sharpened. "Partnership vote is in six months, Lucia. The other partners are watching. These weekend trips to the mountains don't scream dedication."

There it was, the warning she'd been expecting for weeks.

Her hands tightened on the steering wheel. "I've billed more hours than anyone else in my class. The Cannon case is solid. I haven't missed a deadline or a meeting—"

"But you're not here. You're always one foot out the door, heading back to that tiny town." He sighed, and she could picture him in his corner office, looking out over the city with that expression of vague disappointment he wore so well. "Look, I'm not trying to be the bad guy. I'm trying to help you. Partnership means sacrifice. It means putting the firm first. If you're not prepared to do that..."

He let the implication hang.

She stared at the highway stretching ahead, winding into the mountains. Six months ago, even six weeks ago, she'd have immediately reassured him. Would have promised to cancel her trips, to be in the office more, and make whatever sacrifices it took. But that was before Christmas. Before Maddie and Oakley, and learning what it felt like to be part of her family instead of running from it.

"I understand," she said finally. "I'll call you tomorrow to discuss the Cannon prep."

"See that you do." He hung up without saying goodbye.

She exhaled slowly, forcing her shoulders to relax. The city was far behind her now, the landscape shifting to pine forest and rocky cliffs. The late afternoon sun painted everything gold and amber. Despite Richard's warning, she felt some of the tension ease from her chest.

This drive had become familiar over the past few months. After Maddie and Nico's wedding in January, Lucia had started coming back more regularly. At first, it was only once a month, and it was full of uncertainties. Slowly, that turned into every other weekend, and now she was making the trip almost weekly. Each time she was pulled by something she couldn't quite name, or maybe she was afraid to name it.

Her phone buzzed with a text message, and as she came to a red light, she glanced at the screen. Maddie.

> Are you close? I know you said around seven, but I'm hoping you'll be here soon. Having a rough day.

Lucia frowned and typed back one-handed.

> About two hours out. Everything okay?

> Fine. Just tired. Ignore me. Drive safely. Love you.

The casual *love you* still caught Lucia off guard sometimes. Maddie said it so easily, like it was the most natural thing in the world. Like Lucia had always been part of the family instead of the sister who'd run away at eighteen and barely looked back for a decade.

That was changing now. Slow and carefully, she and Nico were rebuilding what had broken between them after their parents died. It wasn't easy. There was far too much history and years of resentment and misunderstandings, but they were trying.

Having Maddie as a sister-in-law helped. Maddie, who somehow saw all the Matthew family dysfunction and decided to stay anyway. Who'd claimed her mate bond with Nico and brought light back into his life.

Lucia pressed down on the accelerator, speeding up slightly.

The miles passed in a blur of pine trees and mountain peaks. She'd grown up in these mountains and knew every curve of this road. Nico had taught her to drive on the switchbacks, and as a teenager, she learned to shift in these forests. Then she'd left it all behind.

Her parents' death had shattered everything. Nico, only twenty-two, had suddenly become the alpha of their clan and her guardian. He had tried to hold everything together. She was seventeen, and suddenly her brother was trying to be her parent, her alpha, and her brother all at once. He'd suffocated her under rules, expectations, and protective instincts.

The day after she turned eighteen, she was on the road to Denver. Thanks to her parents pushing her to dual-enroll in college while still in high school, she'd already completed three years of her undergrad and was accepted into a hybrid program. She'd finish the last year of her bachelor's while starting law school.

Denver seemed to be the perfect place for a new start. She'd built a life that was entirely hers, where nobody expected her to be anything except excellent. It wasn't until recently that she realized excellent also meant lonely.

Lately, driving away from the city has felt more like freedom than moving toward it. She shook off the thought. She had a good life. A career many would kill for, and a great condo with a view. She had respect, success, and independence. She just wished it felt like enough.

Her phone rang again as she crossed over into the town limits. This time, though, it wasn't Richard, it was her brother, Nico.

"Hey," she answered. "I'm literally pulling into town right now."

"Perfect." Her brother's voice was strained. "Are you coming straight to the house?"

Lucia's stomach sank. "What's wrong? Is Maddie—"

"She's fine, so is the baby. She's just..." He exhaled roughly. "Morning sickness has been brutal. She can't keep anything down, and she won't admit she needs help. Oakley's picking up on the stress and acting out. I've got three dozen things that need to happen at the farm before the season starts, and I—" He stopped abruptly.

She had never heard her brother sound so overwhelmed. Nico, who'd been alpha since he was barely more than a kid. Who'd raised Oakley alone after Elena died and carried every responsibility like it was his sacred duty.

"Hold on, Nico, I'm ten minutes away."

She ended the call and drove faster than she should through Main Street, past the general store where Kate waved from the window, past the diner and the small post office, and the town square with its massive pine tree. The town looked like something from a postcard, quaint, cozy, and exactly the kind of place tourists paid good money to visit.

This place used to feel like a prison. Now it felt like...

She refused to finish the thought.

At the end of a long winding driveway, the main house came into view. Smoke curled from the chimney despite the mild October weather. Nico's truck was parked at an angle, as if he'd been in a hurry. The Christmas tree farm stretched out behind the house, rows and rows of evergreens waiting for the season to begin.

She grabbed her overnight bag from the passenger seat and headed for the front door. It opened before her high-heeled boots touched the wooden porch.

Nico looked like he hadn't slept in days. His dark hair was disheveled, his shirt wrinkled, and there were shadows under his amber eyes that hadn't been there last weekend.

"I'm so glad you're here," he said

The statement was direct, but it was the first time in fifteen years her brother had said it and actually meant it. She felt a part deep within her break open. It had been locked tight for too long, and that statement was the final piece to crack it open.

"Where do you need me?" she asked.

He sagged slightly with relief. "Everywhere."

From inside the house, Oakley hollered, her voice high and anxious, "Daddy! Mom needs you."

Nico was already moving, and Lucia followed him inside, dropping her bag by the door.

The house was in chaos. Oakley was standing at the bottom of the stairs, still wearing her school uniform, face scrunched with worry. The kitchen showed evidence of an attempted meal, abandoned ingredients on the counter, and a pot boiling over on the stove.

"I've got the stove," Lucia said, moving toward the kitchen.

Nico nodded and took the stairs two at a time.

In the kitchen, she turned off the burner, wiped up the spill, and then looked at her niece. Oakley had grown so much since Christmas. Her face was losing its baby roundness, her legs getting longer. She'd be tall like Nico.

"Hey, Oak," she said gently. "Rough day?"

Oakley's bottom lip trembled. "Mom's sick again. She won't eat, and Daddy's worried even though he pretends he's not. I asked if the baby was going to make Mom die, like my first mom died, and Daddy got really quiet and weird."

"Oh, honey." She crossed the kitchen toward Oakley and pulled her in for a tight hug. "Your mom isn't going to die. She's just got morning sickness, which is totally normal when you're pregnant. Uncomfortable, but normal."

"Are you sure?"

"I'm sure. Maddie is healthy and strong. Your little brother or sister is just fine in there."

Oakley held tight for another moment before she pulled back. "I'm glad you're here, Aunt Lucia. Everything's better when you're here."

The words hit harder than they should have. This little girl, who barely knew Lucia before Maddie came into their lives, now looked at her like she belonged here. Like she was family. The problem was that Lucia was starting to believe it too.

And I have absolutely no idea what to do about it.

PREVIEW: HOLLOW INHERITANCE

Escaping the city life, Lena Barkstone hopes that Hollow Creek will offer her a quiet space to figure out her next steps. Instead, she finds territorial wolves in her backyard, a tangle of secrets, and a magical battle that all hinges on her.

In the middle of all of it are three magnetic men. Broody Atlas, her best friend's older brother, despises outsiders and wants her out of town. Rowan, the tattooed bartender with a gentle heart he tries to keep hidden. Then there is sweet, quiet Silas, who offers help when she needs it the most.

The unexpected suitors aren't just dangerous for her heart, they're shifters bound by ancient magic. With Samhain looming, the veil between the worlds thins, allowing rogues to enter the human world. Lena is left trusting the wolves she knows, against the ones lurking in the dark forest.

CHAPTER ONE:
HOLLOW GROUND

F og crept along the grounds like long fingers as Lena Barkstone stepped out of her car, directly into a puddle. *Of course.* She stared up at the sagging house that was now hers. It loomed before her as if it regretted having survived yet another year. The paint peeled, and the iron fence bordering the property did nothing to keep out the mist coiling through the overgrowth.

"This is fine," she muttered to herself as she opened the back door before she dragged a cardboard box from the backseat of her car. "This is totally fine. This house isn't trying to eat my soul, it's just old and creaky, not haunted."

The tape at the bottom of the box gave way, sending Halloween lights and decorations tumbling onto the cracked driveway.

"Of course," she said flatly.

Weeks had passed since Aunt Mira's death, and still Lena couldn't decide what to do with the house. Keep it or sell the old house and forget about the note that was left that simply read:

It's yours now. Keep the wards up. Stay away from the woods on All Hallows' Eve.

Whatever that meant.

She hadn't been close to her aunt, but something about the place called to her. Maybe it was the fog. Perhaps it was the fact that she had nothing left in the city but terrible memories and a lease she could barely afford. Or maybe she just needed a place to disappear. Whatever it was, it felt like the fresh start she needed.

Leaning down, she gathered the scattered contents of the box. Hopefully, her day wouldn't continue the same way it started. With everything in her hands, she stood and took a deep breath, filling her lungs with the scent of wet leaves and something earthier. *Home.*

Heading up the old wooden stairs, the house greeted her with a groan, the type that came from the bones of a building, not its walls. Still, the stained-glass windows glowed in the late afternoon light, and the front door opened without protest. Inside, it was dark and chilly, but the structure seemed solid enough.

She just had to look through the dust and neglect to see that the place had potential. There wasn't any doubt in her mind that the house needed work, but with a bit of elbow grease, she'd restore this place to its former glory. It didn't have to be her forever home, but it could provide a place to sort out her life and decide her next step.

Over the next few hours, she unpacked what little she'd brought and fought her way through cobwebs to find a functioning kitchen. It was a bit of a nightmare, but with some work, she'd get it up to standard. The bathroom, on the other hand, reeked of mildew, and she was pretty sure the attic growled at her.

She stepped out onto the porch and scanned the garden. While it was likely once beautiful, it had now become a tangled web of overgrowth. The rose bushes were overtaking the fence, and the stone path had more broken pieces than solid ones. Everything was covered in silence so thick that it made breathing difficult.

Halloween was her favorite time of year, and with the creepy house vibes, she was going to lean into the spooky nature of the season. She pulled out a couple of ceramic jack-o'-lanterns and placed them near the door before setting her sights on the archway leading to the garden. The string of orange lights would be perfect there. As she pulled them from the box, she froze. Her gaze shot up, glancing around the outdoor space. It almost felt as if she were being watched. She stilled, listening. The wind blew, and leaves rustled, but the hairs on the back of her neck didn't lie. Something was out there.

Slowly, she turned toward the woods. Just beyond the cracked stone fence, trees tall and close together, like they'd grown that way just to keep people out. The fog was thicker there, clinging to trunks, winding between roots. Then she saw them.

Eyes. Glowing faintly gold. Low to the ground. Too steady. Not a flicker of reflected light, but something alive. A wolf.

She froze. It was huge. Bigger than any she'd seen. Dark fur with threads of silver mixed in, head low, watching her with predatory stillness.

Slowly, she reached into the pocket of her jeans, pulling out her cell phone. With a flicker of her gaze, she looked at the screen. *Shit! No bars.*

When she looked up again, the wolf was gone.

Just gone. No sound. No movement. As if it had never been there.

"Cool." She let out a shaky laugh. "A hallucination. Love that for me."

Leaving the lights unplugged, she stepped toward the back door. Her gaze was still searching the wood line, as if expecting the wolf to reappear. She needed to get inside. Inside meant safety. At least from wolves. The house, no doubt, had its own safety issues.

Without turning her back to the darkness, she stepped into the house and shut the door behind her. With a quick flip of the deadbolt, she let out a sigh.

"Just a wild animal passing through." Even as she said the words, she didn't believe it.

ABOUT THE AUTHOR

Kelsey Karson is a lifelong romantic who believes love always finds a way, no matter the odds. Married and living with her two dogs, she writes emotionally driven romances that explore forbidden attraction, societal boundaries, and the courage it takes to choose love when the world says you shouldn't. Whether her characters are defying expectations or fighting impossible circumstances, Kelsey's stories celebrate passion, resilience, and the belief that no rule is stronger than the heart. Through her work, she invites readers to believe in love without limits and to let no one else define how or whom you love.

www.KelseyKarson.com

ALSO BY KELSEY KARSON

Hollow Series

Hollow Inheritance

Hollow Anchor

Hollow Threshold

Hollow Pact

Timber Ridge

Christmas with a Bear Shifter

Carved in Timber Ridge

Return to Timber Ridge (October 2026)

Her Mountain Christmas (November 2026)

Stand Alone

Temptation